LOOKING

"Look, have you see[...] Marquez. "I've been c[...]

Austin frowned. "Didn't he say anything to you?"

"About what?" Marquez asked impatiently. She couldn't seem to stop her knees from jiggling.

"He left around six or so. He had his backpack and his sleeping bag—which is to say everything he owns, pretty much. Said something about going camping for a couple of days, getting away from the real world."

Marquez leapt out of her chair like she'd been ejected. "Are you *sure*? He didn't say anything to me, Austin, and I know he would have. And he just started a new job, he's supposed to work tomorrow, this doesn't make any sense." Her pulse throbbed in her throat. She couldn't get enough air. It was like trying to breathe through a straw. "There's something wrong, Austin. He wouldn't just split like this unless something were really, really wrong . . ."

Titles in the MAKING WAVES series

1. Summer can't choose
2. Seth wants more
3. Diana fights back
4. Marquez breaks free
5. Summer's last chance
6. Diana makes a move
7. Looking for Diver
8. Summer loves again

MAKING WAVES

Looking for Diver

KATHERINE APPLEGATE

Pan Books

Cover photography by Jutte Klee

First published 1996 in the United States by Pocket Books

This edition published 1996 by Macmillan Children's Books
a division of Macmillan Publishers Limited
25 Eccleston Place, London SW1W 9NF
and Basingstoke

Associated companies throughout the world

ISBN 0 330 34953 8

1 3 5 7 9 8 6 4 2

A CIP catalogue record for this book is available from
the British Library.

Printed by Mackays of Chatham PLC, Kent

For Michael

1

How Not to Dot Your I's

It was a simple enough note. No question what it meant.

And yet as she held it, the paper shivering slightly between clamped fingers, Diana found herself recalling an article on handwriting analysis she'd read somewhere. One of her mom's *Cosmos*, maybe, something with a title like "Love Letters: How to Read Between His Lines."

Of course, this would technically come under the heading of a "hate letter." And it wasn't from a guy—it was from her cousin.

Diana studied the note again, as if the handful of words had been written in code:

Seth and Diana:
I know everything.

Do not try to get in touch with me.
Summer.

The broad stroke across the *t*. The thick period, almost a dash, after the name. The sharp, hurried writing, nothing like Summer's usual silly, feminine loops. Summer, who'd been known to dot her I's with hearts. Yes, if the handwriting was any indication, Summer was most definitely furious.

That was, after all, what Diana had intended. It hadn't surprised her to come home to the apartment and see Summer's closet half emptied, her suitcase gone.

Everything was going according to plan.

Except for this note. Diana hadn't expected it. The words on paper made everything so permanent and official. She'd felt this way when they'd handed over her driver's license, the plastic coating still a little warm, the picture startled and not quite herself.

This was real. Diana had hurt her cousin in a way she could never take back. She'd wanted to hurt Summer, she'd had her reasons for hurting her, and yet now Diana couldn't take her eyes off the note in her trembling hands.

She heard a key fumbling in the lock. Seth, Summer's boyfriend, came in. He was carrying a package and a bouquet of roses.

"For me?" she asked sarcastically.

"Yeah, right." He tossed the roses aside. "Where's Summer?"

"You tell me." She held out the letter, vaguely noting the way it continued to flutter in her fingers like a trapped moth.

Seth grabbed the paper from her. She watched him take in the words, the permanent, official words, just as she had.

"You *told* her about us?"

"I have no idea how she found out," Diana said, snatching back the note.

Unless, of course, it was the love letter I wrote you, she added silently. *The one I left out so Summer would find it.*

Seth sank against the counter. His lips worked at forming words, but none came. She imagined those lips on her mouth, her neck, remembered the sure and gentle way he had of kissing.

"But how?" Seth said at last. "How could she have found out?"

"The point is, she was going to find out eventually, Seth."

"But not now, not when I finally thought we had things worked out. . . ."

Diana turned toward the sink, away from Seth's wounded eyes. "You've gotten through other stuff. Maybe she'll forgive you for this."

"She'll never forgive either of us."

"I know," Diana admitted. It was a price

she'd been willing to pay to win Seth for good. Lose a cousin, gain a cousin's boyfriend. It had seemed like a reasonable exchange.

"Where do you think she went?" Seth asked.

"She left a note for Marquez. You could read it. Maybe it says something."

Seth marched to Marquez's bedroom. A moment later he returned. "Summer is at that new job of hers, taking care of that handicapped guy. I guess she's staying at his house." He gazed at the peach-colored roses on the counter. "You told her, didn't you?"

Diana didn't answer.

"I thought so."

"She loves Austin, Seth. Why can't you see that?"

"But she *chose* me."

The catch in his voice made her reach for him. She was surprised when he didn't push her away. She kissed him, hoping he might kiss her back, knowing he wouldn't.

"*I* chose you too, Seth," she whispered, pulling away.

"Then you chose wrong." He rubbed his eyes. They were both silent. Through the French doors came the sound of the ocean, sighing again and again over some great, unspeakable loss.

"I was going to head back to California tomorrow," Seth said. "But I can't leave now, not with things like this."

Diana stared at the note in her hand. Things with Summer, he meant. "What about things with . . ." With us, she wanted to say, but of course she didn't.

"With what?"

Diana turned away. Slowly she tore the letter into long, neat strips. She stuffed them into the garbage disposal. She ran the water. With a flick of the switch the disposal chewed up the paper, growling purposefully.

Diana turned off the disposal. She watched the water run. The note was gone, but she could still see the letters in her mind, the tight scrawl, the scribbled signature of the cousin she'd lost forever.

2

Betrayal Is a Mighty Big Word

Summer woke from her nap in a room that was not her own. She blinked. For a brief, terrifying instant she had absolutely no idea where she was. She sat up, taking in the thick oriental rug, the deep blue wallpaper shimmering like satin, the Tiffany lamp sending jeweled patterns onto the ceiling.

Well, wherever she was, she'd clearly come into money.

Oh. She was at her job. Her brand-new, live-in companion job.

She was at her brand-new, live-in companion job because she couldn't ever go home again.

It was amazing, the way you could go to sleep and leave your complicated life completely behind you. Of course, the waking up wasn't much fun.

She walked to the wide pair of doors that opened onto the balcony. It was nearly dark, and the air had a touch of coolness in it. The ocean view was stunning, endless black against a sky of velvety twilight blue, but her eyes were drawn back across the inlet to Coconut Key. The lights along the coast glowed yellow. The old lighthouse at the north end of the key swept its single eye over the dark water.

Running here to Jared's estate had made sense a few hours ago. It was the only place she knew of where she could avoid Seth and Diana indefinitely. And she was going to be working here every day, anyway. One whole wing was filled with assorted staff members.

But now, standing here on the balcony, it seemed crazy, almost pathetic. Summer had never felt quite so thoroughly alone. She was barely on speaking terms with her brother. Her best friend, Marquez, was caught up in her own problems. And Summer had just learned she'd been betrayed by her cousin and her fiancé.

Betrayal. It was a big, dramatic word, like something from her English class on Shakespeare. From the Cliffs Notes, anyway.

She smiled, just a little. It was too much like a soap opera to be her life. Of course, in soap operas the main characters didn't run off to hide and lick their wounds, not unless they were due to be killed off because the ratings were down.

She was surprised at how empty she felt. Shouldn't she be throwing things, vowing revenge, cursing the names of Seth and Diana? In a soap opera she would get even. She would steal Seth back from Diana, she would make Seth pay for his lies. Or at least get amnesia, adopt a new identity, and return to town as a redhead.

But all she felt was emptiness. It almost disappointed her. Was she such a wimp she couldn't even dredge up a decent anger high? Marquez would be outraged on Summer's behalf. Why couldn't Summer manage to feel anything?

She tried to imagine Diana in Seth's arms. Tried to imagine them laughing at how naive Summer was, how they'd faked her out. She felt like a computer in need of a bigger memory. A little more RAM—maybe then she'd see the whole picture. Maybe then she'd come up with the appropriate feelings.

She heard a soft motorized whir and looked down to see Jared, the guy she'd been hired to assist, moving slowly down the long cement path to the beach. He was swathed in bandages—his arms, his face, one leg. The other leg was in a cast.

He paused at the sand's edge, unable to go

farther. He looked so alone, even more alone than Summer. She wondered why his family wasn't here for him. He had no friends, just the people hired to care for him. And now Summer was one of them, his paid companion.

When she'd come running here, suitcase in hand, she'd told Jared what had happened. *For him to have hurt you like this,* he'd said, *he must have truly lost his way.*

Losing your way. It was a nice phrase. It was how she'd felt a lot this summer, since graduating. Lost. Faced with hard choices and no nice neat plan to guide her—just her hunches about what made sense. As if life were one humongous, unsolvable geometry problem. Which college to choose. Which job to take. Which guy to pick—Austin or Seth.

She'd picked Seth. Out of loyalty, and out of love.

So much for hunches.

She went back into the huge bedroom. A large stone fireplace dominated one end of the room, but it was hard to imagine ever using it here in Florida. Around the fireplace dark wood shelves held thick, leather-bound books. She scanned the shelves, found a couple of promising titles, and pulled them out. She'd promised Jared she'd read to him tonight.

Summer headed down the long winding staircase. The house was quiet, as immaculate as a hospital and just about as sterile. Even the perfectly manicured garden in the back seemed antiseptic—not a dying bloom or fallen leaf anywhere.

"Hi, Jared," she said quietly, hoping not to startle him.

He turned his bandaged head an inch or two. Again she was reminded of a mummy. Between the bandages covering his injuries from the car accident, the cast on his leg, and the expensive clothes, the only parts of his body visible were his dark, luminous eyes and his left hand.

"I thought you were napping," he said, in the hoarse whisper caused by his injured vocal cords.

"I was. It was nice too. I sort of forgot everything." She sat on the white bench at the end of the path.

"I do that," Jared said. "Then when I wake up, I'm always sort of shocked by all these bandages."

Summer nodded. His problems were so enormous that she felt her own shrivel in comparison. "I brought *Huckleberry Finn*," she said. "And something about spies I've never heard of. I thought I could read to you, if you want."

Jared stared at her in that unselfconscious way he had, as if she were an expensive museum piece he'd just acquired. "We'll start tomorrow. You relax, sit here. You had a rough day."

"Not so rough."

"Your boyfriend and your cousin—" Jared began, letting the rest go unsaid. "That's pretty rough."

Summer's eyes stung, surprising her with tears. She hadn't cried yet. But the sound of pity in a stranger's voice was like the starting shot she'd been waiting for. She looked away, down the thin white beach. The sky was the vivid, unreal blue of night starting. Gaslights in the garden glowed like huge fireflies.

"I just feel like such a fool," Summer said, still looking away. "How could I not have known there was something between them? I can even understand how Seth might have had feelings for someone else, because I do. Did, I mean. But to keep it from me, all these months . . ."

"Did you tell him?" Jared asked.

Summer turned to face him. He seemed to be straining toward her, leaning in his wheelchair with effort. She wondered if he was so intensely curious because he'd been starved for companionship for many months, or if he was just being polite.

"I told him eventually," she admitted. She managed a weak smile. "I know, I know. How can I be mad at him when I did the same . . . but it's not the same, not really. Diana's my cousin, Jared. For her and Seth to be together—I don't know. It feels different. Like a bigger betrayal."

Again that word. And again she wondered why she couldn't match her sad, small feelings to the big hurt it implied.

"I've done my share of betraying people," Jared said. "It's much easier than you'd think. But cleaning up the mess afterward . . . that isn't so easy." The slight movement around his lips made her wonder if he was smiling.

The glass doors to the back porch eased open, and Summer turned to see Stan, Jared's butler. "A visitor to see Ms. Smith," he said in his clipped New England accent.

"Visitor?" Summer repeated. Marquez! Marquez had gotten her note and rushed over after work to commiserate. Summer felt a surge of relief.

"It's probably my roommate," Summer told Jared. "I hope you don't mind. I mean, we didn't really discuss whether it's okay for me to have guests—"

"Of course," Jared said. "It's your house too, for as long as you want."

She started down the long path that snaked through the garden. Stan was holding the door, waiting so stiffly that she felt a little like royalty. A figure appeared in the dim glow of the porch light. Summer gasped.

"Summer," Seth said. "We have to talk."

3

First Love, First Good-bye

"I have nothing to say to you, Seth."

Seth rushed at her, grabbing her shoulders. His face was grim. "We have to talk. You have to let me explain."

Summer shook off his hands. "Please, Seth," she said.

She was terribly aware of Stan and Jared, perfect strangers watching her private drama unfold. She felt like an actor in a very poorly attended outdoor performance of *General Hospital.*

But Seth was adamant. "I'm not leaving."

"It's all right, Summer," Jared said, rolling toward her down the path. His voice was barely audible over the sound of the waves crashing on the beach. "I was just leaving."

When he reached them, Jared paused for a moment, the hum of his wheelchair suddenly quieted.

"Jared, this is Seth Warner," Summer said.

"Hi." Seth gave a terse nod.

"You okay?" Jared asked Summer.

"Fine. I'm sorry about this. Maybe we can read tomorrow."

"Tomorrow," Jared said. He tilted his head, eyeing Seth carefully, then headed toward the door where Stan was waiting.

Summer returned to the bench and sat stiffly. Seth joined her, careful to leave space between them. She realized suddenly that this could be the last time they saw each other. They would call it off. Seth would go back to California. Down the road they might run into each other—say, at a party for a mutual friend. She could picture the awkward, surprised glance, the cold, heavy feeling in her chest. She wondered if they would even acknowledge each other. Would they pretend all their time together had never happened?

"How did you find out?" Seth asked.

"A love letter. From Diana to you."

He gave a harsh laugh. "I never saw it."

"She never sent it."

"Diana wanted you to find out, you know." Seth was staring at the ocean, not at her. "If we end things over this, it'll be just what she wanted to have happen."

Summer sighed. She had the strange desire to nestle close to him, not because she needed to, but out of habit. It seemed unreal, the two of them sitting there like strangers waiting for a bus.

"I can almost understand you wanting Diana," Summer said. She was surprised at how reasonable she sounded. "I mean, she's beautiful and smart and sexy and . . ."

"Not you," Seth finished. "She's not you, Summer."

"Maybe that was the whole point."

"There was no 'point,' it was just an . . . an accident. I didn't mean for it to happen—"

"Were you . . . together when she went out to California last week to visit?"

Seth squirmed a little. "We saw each other, yeah."

"Were you *together?*" Summer pressed.

He didn't answer. Well, duh, Summer. Connect the dots. She'd actually been naive enough to encourage Diana to visit Seth. They must have had a good laugh over that. Summer Smith, junior matchmaker.

"As I was saying," Summer continued in a prim lecturing voice that she'd never heard from herself before, "I could almost understand your going after Diana. The temptation and all. It's like Austin and me." She was glad when he winced a little. "But what I can't understand, Seth, is how you could have kept it from me all these months. How you could have let me feel so rotten and guilty about Austin when you knew what you'd done with Diana was every bit as bad. Worse, even."

"Why is it any worse?" Seth asked. "Why isn't it just the same?"

"I can't explain it—it just is. Because she's my cousin and my roommate, and you knew, you *both* knew, how much it would hurt me."

"You hurt me too, Summer. And I forgave you."

"Do you love Diana?"

"No," Seth said automatically. "Not exactly."

"Not exactly."

"I'm only *in* love with you. Doesn't that make it any better, Summer?"

"In a way it makes it worse, Seth. Because it means you were just using Diana. It makes me feel sorry for her."

"The using was mutual, trust me. You don't need to feel sorry for Diana. You think it was an accident I flew back here to see you? Diana's the one who told me you weren't wearing my ring anymore. She's the one who told me about Austin—" His voice cracked.

She watched the tears trail down his cheeks. It scared her how indifferent she felt. How numb. She'd only seen Seth cry a couple of times. But now, seeing him cry over her, it was like watching a movie where you'd already figured out the ending and you wondered if maybe you should go buy some more popcorn.

"Summer." Seth took her hand. "We can't let it end like this. This is crazy. We've been through too much together. We're engaged."

"We *were* engaged."

"What about everything you said last night?" Seth cried. He was growing increasingly frantic, but the more agitated he got, the more cool and centered she felt. "About how what mattered most was loyalty and faithfulness and all we'd gone through together? Are you telling me this is it? It's over?"

Summer thought for a while. The finality of it all began to penetrate, like a tiny flashlight in dense fog. "It just feels like we've gone through too much, Seth," she said softly. "It's like . . . like that car of yours that you finally sold to the junkyard for parts. That Dodge? Remember how you kept trying to patch it together and as soon as you did something else would go wrong—the back door fell off or the alternator died? And then that old man rear-ended you in the parking lot at Wendy's and you just said, okay, it's time to give up. This is like the final straw. This is our rear-ending at Wendy's."

She tried to smile, but the muscles wouldn't obey. It occurred to her that only a few days ago, she'd told Austin it was over between them. In the space of a week she'd ended relationships with the two great loves of her life.

Last summer she'd come to the Keys just hoping to meet a cute guy, maybe even fall in love. She'd worried about her flirting technique and her dancing technique and her kissing technique.

And now here she was, polishing her breaking-up technique.

Suddenly she felt very old. Older than Seth. Older than her friends. Older even than those actors on *90210.*

Seth reached into his pocket. He held out something small and shiny in his palm, and she knew at once that it was another ring.

"I found it at Woolworth's today," Seth said. "A replacement ring for your replacement ring." He paused. "When Diana came to see me in California, she brought a ring with her. She said it was yours."

Summer gasped. "*She* found my ring and didn't tell me?"

"I was going to mail the real one to you when I got back to California. But now I guess you won't be needing it."

"No," Summer said softly.

Seth pressed the ring into her hand. "You might as well take this. I've already got a real one. Besides, I'm not going back to California for a while."

"What? You have to go back and finish your internship. You said you were learning so much about boat building—"

"Screw all that. I'm going to go hang out with my grandfather on Crab Claw for a while. Finish up the summer there."

"Look, there's something you should know, Seth. I reapplied to Carlson College."

Seth looked at her blankly. "When?"

"Before this. Before I found out about you and Diana. I went for a visit, and I realized I was only going to UW to please you. Well, mostly I realized I was going there because I was afraid I couldn't hack it at Carlson."

"I thought you wanted us to be together. So you were planning on breaking up with me all along?"

"No, no. I knew it was going to be hard, being at different colleges, but I thought you could try to reapply to Carlson next semester and—"

"What does it matter now?" Seth interrupted. "The point is, you were ready to give up on us."

"No." Summer closed her fingers around the little ring with its fake diamond. "I just wasn't ready to give up on myself. And you shouldn't be either. You should go back to California, finish out the internship."

Seth just shook his head.

"I'm glad for everything we had, Seth." Summer touched his damp cheek. "You'll always be my first love." She was glad she was being so generous. She didn't want to feel bad about this later. No scenes, no accusations.

"Maybe if we give it some time?" Seth said hoarsely.

She started to say, No, it's over, it's time for you to move on. But when she looked into his desperate, regretful eyes, she couldn't bring herself to say it.

"I don't know," she whispered. "Maybe."

The word was so small and sad, so pathetically hopeful. When Seth leaned over and softly kissed her, she felt something inside shift and crack.

She was almost relieved when she finally started to cry herself.

4

Please Leave a Message After the Beep. . . .

Marquez marched down the sidewalk toward her boyfriend's apartment, her dark curls bouncing rhythmically. She'd been calling Diver all evening without success. Now she was opting for the up-close-and-personal approach.

Her mind was reeling. After work she'd gone home to her apartment to change clothes, only to discover that Summer, her best friend, had moved out. Marquez didn't need a scorecard. She'd known all about the little game Diana and Seth had been playing, but she'd kept her mouth shut, hoping things would work out on their own.

Great. Marquez's boyfriend was AWOL, and her best friend had run away from home. It was not a pretty picture.

She climbed the porch steps to the apartment Diver shared with Austin Shaw. Her hand was trembling, but she couldn't tell if it was from nerves or because she hadn't eaten anything all day.

She knocked. "Enter at your own risk," Austin yelled.

Marquez pushed open the door. The room was dense with smoke. Discarded potato chip bags and bottles littered the floor. A tiny fan on a TV tray herded the thick air back and forth.

Austin was lying on the couch, ratty jeans, no shirt. He was reading a *TV Guide.* His half-grown beard was dark against his drawn face. His long brown hair hadn't seen a comb in many a moon. He always looked a little edgy—now he looked downright scuzzy. Still, Marquez could understand why Summer was so taken with him. Even when scuzzy, he was attractively scuzzy.

"Hey, Marquez, join the party. You're just in time. I've got *Doctor Quinn, Medicine Woman* on tape."

Marquez waved her arms to clear the air. "Since when do you smoke?"

"I don't. I'm just experimenting with self-destructive behaviors. Next I thought I'd try the all-doughnut diet. Or else take up skydiving. Of course, that would require moving off the couch, and I think I may be permanently stuck here.

I sat on a package of Oreos a few days back."

"Blythe told me you were late to work and McNair almost fired your butt."

"Yeah. I was very disappointed when he gave me a second chance to clean up my act."

Marquez cleared a spot off a chair and sat. "This is because Summer ended things, huh?"

"I know it's not very melodramatic, eating and drinking myself into a stupor and watching the Weather Channel. I ought to have the decency to fall on my sword or something."

"You may want to hold off on the sword. Summer and Seth just officially broke up. You heard it here first. Look, have you seen Diver anywhere? I've been calling all day—"

"I turned the sound on the machine off." Austin tossed his *TV Guide* to the floor. "Tell me more about this alleged breakup."

"First things first. Diver?"

Austin frowned. "Didn't he say anything to you?"

"About what?" Marquez asked impatiently. She couldn't seem to stop her knees from jiggling.

"He left around six or so. He had his backpack and his sleeping bag—which is to say everything he owns, pretty much. Said something about going camping for a couple of days, getting away from the real world."

Marquez leapt out of her chair like she'd

been ejected. "Are you *sure?* He didn't say anything to me, Austin, and I know he would have. And he just started a new job, he's supposed to work tomorrow, this doesn't make any sense—"

"Whoa, calm down, Marquez." Austin sat up. "I'm sure there's a logical explanation. I did ask him about his job and he said they were cool with it."

"How could they be cool with it? *I'm* not even cool with it!" She grabbed his phone. "Can I use this?"

"Sure."

Marquez hesitated. "Damn. What's his boss's name? Linda something. Linda . . . Linda . . ." She pounded the receiver in her palm.

"Calm down, girl. You sneaking into the double espressos again at Jitters?"

"Linda Right? Linda—"

"Rice?" Austin ventured.

"That's it!" Marquez dialed information, got the number, and waited impatiently for the phone to ring.

"So anyway, about this Summer-Seth situation—" Austin tried, but she ignored him.

"Linda?" she said when a woman answered. "This is Marquez—uh, Maria Marquez, Diver Smith's girlfriend? I'm really sorry to bug you like this, but I was wondering if you could tell me if he's scheduled to work tomorrow."

Marquez listened, said thanks, hung up, and

groaned. "He's scheduled for the next four days straight. She didn't know anything." She wrung her hands. Her pulse throbbed in her throat. She couldn't get enough air. It was like trying to breathe through a straw. "There's something wrong, Austin. He wouldn't just split like this unless something were really, really wrong."

Austin put out his cigarette and stood a little unsteadily. He put his arm around her. "Relax, kid. Nothing's wrong. Now, come here and sit down. Watch those Oreos. I'm getting you some water." He led her to the couch. "Take it easy, Marquez. You've had a hard week. I mean, you just got out of the hospital a little while ago."

She nodded, touching the Band-Aid covering her stitches. She'd felt a little like this that night—dizzy, lost. The diet pills, probably, or not eating. She'd hit her head, fallen.

"Austin, Diver tells me everything. He wouldn't just vanish unless something horrible had happened. You've got to think. Did he say anything else? Leave a note, anything?"

Austin handed her a plastic cup from Burger King filled with water. "I don't think so, Marquez."

"Did he seem okay?"

"Well, I don't know Diver that well. He's always sort of . . . cryptic. But he did look a little down." He sat down next to Marquez. "You know, he did say something weird. A message he wanted me to pass along—"

"To me?"

"To Summer, actually. He said something like, 'Tell Summer she was right about me all along.' Does that mean anything to you?"

Marquez closed her eyes. "It means he wasn't feeling good about himself, I can tell you that much. Summer's not exactly her brother's biggest fan. She blames him for her parents splitting up, for running out on her family—"

Running out. As soon as she said the words, Marquez realized the truth.

Diver, who had spent his life running from problems, could be running once again.

Without thinking, she reached for Austin's hand. He held tight and pulled her close. "He would never run out on you, Marquez. He loves you completely."

"How do you know that?"

"Because he told me so. In that Diver way he has. Said you were the only woman who didn't disturb his *wa*. Whatever the hell that is."

She leaned her head on Austin's warm shoulder. The room was swimming in lazy circles around her. She had to clear her head, get organized. First she'd go see Summer, see if she knew anything. Then . . . well, she'd deal with then when she got there.

"Maybe he tried to call," Austin suggested.

He reached for the answering machine on the floor, his arm still around Marquez.

The first four messages were all from Marquez. *Diver, where are you? Diver, call me. Diver, you said you were going to meet me after work. Damn it, Diver, where* are *you?*

The next was from their boss at Jitters, reminding Austin he'd better be on time for his shift tomorrow.

Then came the last one. *Diver, hon. I* so *enjoyed our little visit this afternoon. Can't wait to see what develops.*

That was it. No name, no number.

"That southern accent," Austin said. "That's got to be Caroline."

Marquez didn't have to be told. She'd watched Diver at the beach party last night, eyeing beautiful, blond, petite Caroline like a lovesick puppy. She'd seen the looks they'd exchanged, and she'd known what they'd meant.

And now Diver and Caroline had spent the afternoon together. "His leaving," Marquez whispered. "It's about Caroline, I know it is."

"Marquez, my darling, crazed Marquez," Austin said, planting a kiss on her cheek, "that frothy little southern magnolia can't hold a candle to you. Diver loves you."

Marquez looked at him. "Yeah, and Summer loved you," she said gently.

Austin gave a crooked smile. "You're making comforting you extremely challenging."

For a moment they sat together, considering their shared plight. At last Austin rose. "Come on. We'll go talk to Summer, see if she knows anything."

"I doubt Summer's in the mood for visitors right now, Austin."

"You can tell me all about it on the way. But first let me brush my teeth, assuming I remember how."

"A little Right Guard wouldn't hurt either."

He laughed. She watched him disappear into the bathroom. When he closed the door, she replayed Caroline's message on the machine. She listened for meaning, for clues in the sweet, musical lilt of Caroline's voice.

But there was nothing there to hear, no matter how hard she tried.

5

It's a Dog of a Way to Get Around

It never hurt in the dream. The sizzling embers under his bare feet were as cool as wet stones. The fire licked at his skin, the fumes poisoned his lungs, but he couldn't feel a thing.

As the fire ate it away, Diver walked through the crumbling house until he found his father, his father who was not really his father, lying under a burning support beam. His clothes were on fire, his hair, even his skin. His mouth was contorted with pain.

He was screaming, but Diver couldn't hear him.

The dream shifted jerkily, like a badly spliced film. He was lying on the ground outside the house now, the fire behind him. The grass was damp and springy against his cheek. His head was bleeding.

He looked back. The fire was like a living thing. He heard sirens howling.

Somewhere nearby he saw a light come on. A shadow passed by a window.

He climbed to his feet and ran, the way he always did in the dream. He was moving wildly, propelled by fear and by the sound of his father's screams that now, at last, he could hear.

He turned the corner down the dark street. The sirens and the screams filled his head. And then, out of the corner of his eye, he saw the hand—a girl's hand, familiar and yet not, reaching out to him. The hand extended from the doorway of an old, rickety house. The house seemed to float over a blue, endless ocean.

The sirens grew louder, the screams tore at him, and then Diver reached for the hand.

Something shook him hard. A voice penetrated through the screams. "Wake up, man."

Diver's eyes flew open. He saw a beefy forearm layered with blue tattoos.

He was on the Greyhound. It was night. He was headed for Miami, or somewhere like that.

"You musta been havin' a nightmare, man." The owner of the tattoos returned to his seat on the other side of the dark aisle.

"Yeah." Diver ran his fingers through long, blond hair. "I guess."

"I get those real bad, man." The tattooed man shrugged. "Course, I'm usually awake."

When the Greyhound made a stop just south of Miami, Diver was grateful for the chance to stretch his legs. It was a seedy building, low-slung and dirty, with a small twenty-four-hour restaurant attached to one end.

With his fellow passengers, groggy and grumbling, Diver shuffled off the bus. The driver leaned against the bus, sucking alternately on a Coke and a cigarette, looking as bleary as the rest of them.

Inside, most of the passengers headed for the restaurant, which smelled of grease and bus fumes. But Diver found himself making his way toward the telephones, old-fashioned booths with accordion glass doors. He entered one, sat on the wooden stool, and held the receiver, still warm from its last use.

He wanted so much to call her. Just to hear Marquez's voice—hear her bitch at him and laugh at him and tell him how she didn't care what was wrong, just please get his butt home.

He could call, let her answer, hang up.

But she would know who it was. By now she was probably pretty worried. It would be wrong, cruel even, to call her like that.

As if running away from her without a word was somehow kind. He leaned against the glass. He felt something low in his chest, a tight place he associated vaguely with anger. He hadn't been angry much in his life. He hadn't felt much at all, actually.

His head hurt the way it had hurt in the dream. As if the dream had been real.

He laughed grimly. Of course, it had been.

He punched 411 into the keypad. "Directory assistance," a man answered.

"I need the number for Blythe, uh . . ." What *was* Caroline's roommate's last name? "Blythe Barrett, I think, in Coconut Key."

"Checking."

He waited, flashing back to his visit from Caroline this afternoon. *I didn't kill him,* he'd told her, but she'd known it wasn't true, and so had he.

The operator gave him the number. He listened to the dial tone hum. What could he say? *Yes, Caroline, you're right. I did kill him. I burned down the house with my father in it and then I ran like hell. Like I'm running now, so fast you'll never find me.*

He hung up the receiver. What was the etiquette when you were running from your blackmailer? Probably it would not be in your best interest to call and taunt her.

He was hungry. He wasn't thinking clearly.

He left the phone booth and went to the restaurant. His fellow travelers were camped out, each in separate booths, sullenly munching down day-old fries and burgers. Diver bought an apple and a granola bar and went outside.

The night wrapped itself around him, warm

and damp. The bus was idling, filling the air with acrid smoke. Above the big windshield a sign glowed red. Miami.

He didn't have much cash. It wasn't the first time. After the fire he'd changed his name and lived on the streets. He could do it again, but the thought of dodging cops and sleazebags and dopers made him deeply tired. He could pick up odd jobs, get by. But he'd liked his last couple of jobs, taking care of injured wildlife at rehab centers. Lousy pay, great work.

A while back Summer had told him he had to get his act together, stop drifting, reacting. Grow up. He really had. He had a job, a place to stay with a roof and four walls, and, of course, his relationship with Marquez.

But a chance meeting with a girl named Caroline had ripped all that from his grasp.

He'd had lunch with Summer just today. It had been tense, like it always was between them these days. But there'd been a moment when she'd reached for his hand and he'd told his sister how much he loved her. At least, he'd told her in his way. He hadn't exactly said the words.

He wolfed down the granola bar. It surprised him a little, the way he could still have an appetite while his life crumbled around him. How had Marquez starved herself all these months? Hoarding calories like gold, exercising to exhaustion, sneaking diet pills. He should have watched out for her better. He should have made her see how beautiful and perfect she was.

And now there was no one to tell her that.

One by one the other passengers returned to the bus. The driver tossed his cigarette. "Time to go, bud," he said.

Diver watched him climb the steps. The engine revved. If he got back on that bus, he'd fall asleep.

If he fell asleep, he'd dream again.

He waved the driver on. The doors squealed shut. The bus slowly pulled away.

The fire, the smoke, the screams would have to wait, for a few more hours at least.

6

A Little Night Visiting

Tap. Taptaptap. Tap.

For the second time in one evening Summer awoke in a room that she didn't recognize. This time, though, it didn't take her as long to remember that she was at Jared's—or to remember why.

She checked the glowing digital clock. It was a little after midnight.

Tap. Taptap. Taptap.

Was it hailing? South Florida was famous for its sudden storms, but when she'd been outside with Seth and Jared, the sky had been clear. And why hadn't she heard any thunder or rain?

She climbed out of bed and went to the window. As she pulled back the curtain the sharp clatter of stones against glass made her jump in surprise. She opened the window.

"Summer! It's me, Marquez!"

"Marquez?" Summer called. "Who's that with you?"

"But, soft!" came a male voice, "what light through yonder window breaks?"

"Austin? What are you doing here?"

"Auditioning for summer stock."

"Let us in, okay?" Marquez called.

"Wait there."

Summer threw on the robe she'd remembered to pack at the last minute. The hallway was dark. Silently she swept down the wide staircase.

Marquez. It would be so good to see Marquez.

She didn't let herself think about how it would be to see Austin.

It took her two tries to disarm the door alarm the way Juanita, Jared's nurse, had taught her before Summer went to bed.

Marquez and Austin were waiting on the wide porch. Summer pulled them in, enforcing silence with a finger to her lips. She led them upstairs to her room and shut the door.

"Be very quiet or they'll fire me for sure," she said in a whisper.

Marquez flew into her arms. "Summer, are you okay? I was so worried when you just left behind that note, and now with Diver—"

"What *about* Diver?"

Marquez burst into tears. Summer looked over at Austin, who was scanning the bookshelves. "Austin? What happened?"

He turned to her, his face grave. "He's gone, Summer."

"Gone?"

Marquez was sobbing—great gasping sounds that Summer had never heard her friend make before.

"This evening I ran into him as he was leaving my apartment," Austin said. "He said he was taking a couple of days off, and that they were cool with it at work."

"B-bu-but I called his job," Marquez sobbed. "And th-th-th—"

"They didn't know anything about it," Austin finished gently.

Summer led Marquez to the bed. They sat there together, Summer's arm draped over her friend's frail shoulders.

"I just saw him this afternoon," Summer said. "He was sort of down, but he didn't mention anything to me." She shook her head. "This would be just like Diver, to run out without a word. It wouldn't exactly be the first time. He didn't even leave a note, nothing?"

Marquez shook her head and sniffled. "But I know why he left. It's that Caroline girl. She left a message on Austin's machine. They got together today, and at the beach last night he couldn't take his eyes off her."

"Marquez," Austin interrupted, "Diver is not interested in Caroline. He's in love with you."

"Diver told me about her, Marquez," Summer said. "He and Caroline were neighbors when they were kids, that's all."

Marquez looked at her hopefully. "Really?"

"He told me at lunch."

"Still, he had to leave for some reason. . . ." Marquez's voice faded away.

"Damn it," Summer muttered, all her pent-up anger at Diver resurfacing. "How could he just walk out like this? I mean, before, when he left Minnesota, I could almost understand. It was a new place, and my family was new to him. It was a hard adjustment, sure. But *now?* Now, when everything's going so well? He has a cool job, and he has you—"

She paused, suddenly aware of her rising voice and of Marquez's soft sobs. There was no point in making things worse. "Marquez, you know Diver," Summer said, softening her tone. "He gets these whims. He's probably sleeping on the beach, doing his back-to-nature thing. Truth is"—she forced a laugh—"he probably couldn't hack living in a normal apartment with Austin."

"Wouldn't be the first roommate I've driven out," Austin agreed.

"And after all," Summer added, "before this, Diver was living in a tree house. He's not like other guys, Marquez. He's got this wild streak in him. He's sort of, well . . . uncivilized. Give him a couple of days without indoor plumbing or remote controls and he'll be back, good as new."

"You think?" Marquez asked.

"I know. He *is* my brother, after all."

"Still"—Marquez grabbed a Kleenex box off Summer's nightstand—"he should have told me. At least when you ran out, you left a note."

"Interesting," Austin noted as he thumbed through a thick book he'd pulled off the shelves. "You both pull a disappearing act on the same day. Perhaps this tendency to vanish runs in the family."

"I did not pull a disappearing act," Summer said sharply. "I was offered a live-in position and I chose to . . . to exercise that option. That's all."

"And what exactly prompted this . . . exercising?" Austin asked, smiling just enough to tell Summer he'd heard about her and Seth.

Summer sighed heavily. "Austin, if you already know about Seth and me, why are you asking? And since we're getting personal, there's this newfangled invention on the market. It's called a razor. I've got one in my bathroom you could borrow, but I've already used it on my legs."

"Actually, that might be very exciting for me."

She turned her attention back to Marquez. "Are you going to be okay tonight?"

Marquez nodded. "I just feel so . . . you know, helpless."

"Tomorrow's your counseling session at the hospital, right?"

Marquez gave a terse nod.

"Well, I'll try to get off early here and when you're done at your session, we'll go on an all-out Diver search. We'll check all the beaches, talk to anyone who might have seen him. We'll track him down, Marquez, I promise. Who knows? He'll probably show up tomorrow, all happy and Zen again, before we can even start looking."

Marquez smiled with one corner of her mouth. "Yeah. That would be Diver, all right." She stood shakily, bracing herself on Summer's shoulder. "Well, we should get going. Nice place, by the way. I can see why you prefer it."

"How'd you find my room, anyway?"

"Process of elimination," Austin answered. "You had the lousiest view."

"It's not fair to leave me alone with Diana, you know," Marquez said. "I had to hide all the sharp knives."

"I know. But I just can't deal with her and Seth right now."

"We've been so busy talking about Diver. You sure you're holding up okay?"

Summer shrugged. Out of the corner of her eye she could see Austin watching her intently. "Just kind of numb."

Marquez looked down at her feet. "Summer. There's something I have to tell you. I, uh, I kind of knew."

Summer blinked. "Knew. You knew what?"

"Don't make this any harder than it already is. I knew about Diana and Seth. I saw this letter from her to him. Really nauseating stuff. I didn't tell you because I thought maybe it was over and I didn't want to mess things up between you and Seth. . . ." She rolled her eyes. "And now look. As usual, with my incredible insight into human nature, I've totally screwed things up. No wonder Diver ran off."

She started to sob again. Summer felt the choices rolling around inside her—yell, cry, be disappointed, be sad. But when she looked at Marquez, so frail and desperate, all she could do was hug her close. "It's okay," she said. "I probably would have done the same thing."

Austin put a gentle hand on Marquez's shoulder. "Come on, kid. How about you and me stop by I Scream? They're open till one, I think. I'll buy you a hot fudge sundae with Reese's Pieces."

"I'm not hungry," Marquez murmured.

"I know," Austin said. "But let's go, anyway. I wouldn't mind some company."

Marquez looked from Summer to Austin and back again. "I need some air," she said. "And I have the feeling you two need some too. I'll meet you downstairs, Austin."

When Marquez was gone, Austin looked a little uncomfortable. "About last night," he said, clearing his throat. "When I crashed your little beach party . . . I believe I may have been slightly inebriated."

"You lay on the beach and made sand angels. It took two of us to drag you home. I'd say 'slightly' was a slight understatement."

Austin winced. "In any case, thanks for lugging me home. And I apologize for my boorish behavior."

"Apology accepted."

"If you need help with Diver . . ."

"Thanks. I'll let you know."

Austin moved a little closer. He touched her hair and she shivered. "About you and Seth—" he began.

"Marquez is waiting," Summer said. "You should probably go."

Austin seemed to be debating whether to press on. "All right," he said at last. "We'll do this another time." He gave her a gentle kiss on the cheek. "You've got enough to deal with right now."

7

Jared's Future, Jared's Past

"Glad you could join us."

Juanita was sitting in the breakfast room, a sunny, spacious area apparently reserved for the staff. She was just a few years older than Summer, a pretty olive-skinned woman with a halo of brown curls. As usual, she was dressed in a crisp white uniform. She sat at the table by a bank of windows overlooking the ocean, removing sections from a grapefruit with systematic care.

"I kind of overslept a little," Summer said apologetically.

"Deb, our cook, is out shopping, so you're on your own," Juanita said. "There's cereal over there in the cupboard by the sink, English muffins by the toaster. Make yourself at home."

Fumbling around in the huge, shiny kitchen, Summer managed to fix herself a bowl of Cheerios. She sat across from Juanita, feeling like an unwanted guest in a near-empty hotel.

"We were supposed to meet at nine to discuss Jared's therapy," Juanita said, opening a notebook.

"I'm really sorry—"

"But before we start, perhaps we should establish some ground rules," she continued. "Jared's family arranged for him to recover here so that he could have complete quiet. Jared's very generous with the staff. We're allowed to have guests and to use the grounds." She paused. "But that does not mean taking advantage of the situation. That does not mean, for example, having one's friends sneak into Jared's home in the middle of the night."

Summer gulped.

"By my count, you've already been visited by three friends, two of them"—she lowered her voice—"*male*. You're obviously a very pretty girl, Summer, and it's only natural that you would have . . . admirers. Including Jared, I suspect." She added the last part as if it were clearly a topic for *Unsolved Mysteries*. "But it is extremely detrimental to his recovery to be reminded of all he's lost. He's just a little older than you are, Summer. Imagine how hard it is for him to be around people his own age, living their normal lives." She paused to sip her tea. "I've spoken to Jared's mother on the phone. Apparently Jared was quite a handsome guy. She said he had no shortage of girlfriends. One in particular he was quite smitten with."

"I wonder where she is."

Juanita shrugged. "I've seen it before. People have an accident like this, it really separates the wheat from the chaff. So-called friends just vanish."

"Poor Jared," Summer said. "I'm truly sorry about my friends coming by. I promise to be more careful in the future."

Juanita smiled. "I'm glad we understand each other." She tore out a page from her notebook. "Now, I've put together a list of therapeutic activities. Jared's been going through a slump. He's very depressed, very uninterested in life. Most of the time he just stares blankly at the TV. Your goal is to help him reengage." She passed the list to Summer.

Summer scanned the section headed "8:00 A.M. to 12:00 P.M." "Wake at eight," she read. "Bathe, change dressings, eight to eight-thirty. Breakfast, eight-thirty to nine. Read newspapers, nine to nine-thirty. Read novels, nine-thirty to ten. Play chess or other board game, ten to eleven—" She frowned. "I know I'm not a nurse or anything, but isn't this kind of . . . you know, regimented?"

She heard a whirring noise behind her, the sound of Jared's motorized wheelchair as he sped into the room. He was neatly dressed as always, in a crisp tailored blue shirt and khaki pants, hemmed at the knee on one side to accommodate his large cast. He had a heavy gold ring on his left hand, and on his good foot he wore an expensive-looking dark leather shoe—attempts, it seemed, to impose order onto the chaos of bandages and plaster.

"She's right," Jared said in his low, gravelly voice. "It does sound regimented." He rolled over to the table and cocked his head to read the list. "My entire future laid out before me." He narrowed his eyes. "What? You didn't bother to schedule in my breathing, Juanita?"

"I just thought a plan of activities would give you something to look forward to each day—"

"We'll wing it, right, Summer?"

"Sure," Summer said. "How about a walk around the neighborhood? A roll, I guess I should say?"

"Fine idea," Jared said.

"I'm not so sure that's advisable, Summer," Juanita said. "Jared's wheelchair is cumbersome, and the temperature is so high—"

"Relax," Jared said. "What's the worst that can happen?"

"The worst that can happen is your throttle will stick and you'll roll straight into the ocean," Juanita said with a reluctant smile.

"I'll take my chances," Jared said.

"Ready?" Summer asked, spooning down the last of her cereal.

"Wear your Nikes. I'm hard to keep up with," Jared advised.

Summer took her bowl to the sink. "There's one thing," she said. "I was sort of wondering if I could have a couple of hours off this afternoon."

"Of course," Jared said, but Juanita was scowling.

"It's this family emergency. My brother's sort of disappeared—"

"Diver's gone?" Jared asked.

"Yeah, he . . . how'd you know his name?"

"You mentioned him yesterday."

"I did? Oh, well, I guess I did. Yesterday's sort of a blur. Anyway, it's probably nothing, he's sort of flaky sometimes, but I was going to help his girlfriend try to track him down."

"No problem," Jared said.

"You seem to lead a very turbulent life," Juanita commented.

"Sometimes I do feel a little seasick," Summer said with a grim smile.

Jared wheeled to his bedroom and closed the door. He pulled his sunglasses out of his nightstand drawer and tucked them in his pocket. Summer was waiting in the foyer to start their walk.

Summer was waiting for him.

Summer.

With great difficulty he removed the burled walnut box he kept at the back of the drawer. He set it on the bed, then wheeled over to the closet. With his good hand he removed the key he'd tucked inside his tennis racket cover.

It was an elaborate precaution, but one he felt was necessary. Juanita respected his privacy, such as it was. But it was too easy to imagine her coming across the box and inspecting its contents.

He locked his bedroom door and returned to the bed. It took three tries, but he was finally able to twist the key. The catch released. Slowly Jared opened the lid.

The picture was on top, where he'd left it. A beautiful girl on a sailboat, blond hair shimmering in the Florida sun, smiling radiantly at the camera. A handsome young man, dark eyed and too cocky, his arm draped around her shoulders.

He touched his bandaged face. He hadn't been such a bad-looking guy, all things considered.

Of course, that was a year ago. A lifetime ago. Back when he'd actually thought he might someday hear Summer say, *I love you, Adam.* Back when he'd been the rich son of a powerful senator. Back when everything he wanted came with such sweet ease he'd never imagined life could be any other way.

He was still rich. But his father had retired from the Senate in disgrace. His brother, Ross, was dead.

And he wasn't the cocky guy on the sailboat anymore, the guy who was sure Summer would fall in love with him, like every other girl he'd ever wanted.

Summer had been different. Summer, *he'd* loved.

That had only happened to him once before.

He pulled another picture out of the box. A girl on the beach, hiding behind dark sunglasses. She was Summer's opposite, dark, complicated, her smile full of secrets, and yet they shared one important quality—they both believed in love in a way he never had and never could. He'd believed in loyalty. Family above all else. And he'd lost both girls because of it.

He put back the pictures, locked the box, hid the key. A knock at the door startled him.

"Jared?" Juanita asked. "You need any help?"

"I'm fine. Tell Summer I'll be right there."

He returned the box to its hiding place. He should tell Summer who he was, of course. This couldn't go on forever. But he didn't want to.

For today, at least, for right now, Summer was waiting for him.

Summer.

8

Nice People and Not So Nice

The sign on the door was small, handwritten. Eating Disorders Clinic.

For the third time Marquez walked past the door, casually, indifferently. The hospital, even this part, the outpatient wing, stank of disinfectant. It was making her woozy and lightheaded. Or maybe it was the fact that she hadn't eaten in ages.

She headed for the lobby and sank into a chair. She should go home, work her shift at Jitters, then try to look for Diver. She and Summer could start with the beaches north of town. He liked those. She could imagine him baking in the sun, his shades hiding innocent baby blues, grinning when she finally tracked him down. He'd show her some shell he'd found, or some injured pelican, or whatever had distracted him from acting like a normal human being and telling her where he was.

That was the good version.

In the bad version, the R-rated one that had kept her up all night, he was having a secret rendezvous with Caroline. Marquez wasn't exactly sure where or how, but she knew why. He was with Caroline because she was everything Marquez wasn't: beautiful, petite, thin.

A nurse walked by, rustling in her uniform. She paused, glancing down the hall at the ED door and then back at Marquez.

"Can I help you with directions?" she asked.

"I'm just . . . you know. Waiting for someone."

"At the ED Clinic?" She had a nice smile. Nice, but nosy.

Marquez reached for an aging *People* magazine to prove she really was waiting. "Yeah. She's in there. Jane. She's, um, one of those throwing-up people."

"Bulimic?"

"I guess. Me, I could never do that. I despise throwing up."

The nurse stared. Marquez looked down at her magazine. David Hasselhoff was on the cover. He looked very tan and very old.

"Well, they're nice people at the clinic," the nurse said gently. "I'm sure she'll like it there. They really know how to listen."

"She's not very talkative," Marquez said.

"They'll understand. Tell her to give it a chance."

"Yeah. I'll try. But she doesn't really listen to me."

"There's a counselor on staff here all the time," the nurse said. "You might pass that along."

Marquez flipped through the worn pages of her magazine.

"If you get thirsty, there's a machine down the hall," the nurse said, smiling that sympathetic smile again. "While you wait."

Marquez watched her leave. She was average weight, maybe a little big in the hips, probably some cellulite on the thighs. But still. Nothing like Marquez. Marquez, who made Shamu look like a runway model.

She stared down the hall, imagining the other girls behind the ED door. If she tried hard enough, she could almost believe the lie she'd told the nurse. She was just waiting for Jane. Jane, who was a pretty messed-up girl, who threw up breakfast so she could have another one.

She lingered over an article on some supermodels in L.A. who'd started a new restaurant. In a big color photo they were grouped around a table overflowing with food, enough calories to keep them all happy for a year. One of them, a model Marquez had seen on the covers of

Seventeen and *Mademoiselle,* had a french fry poised delicately between perfectly manicured nails. Of course, she probably barfed it up after the photo shoot. They all did it.

Marquez had seen girls at school do it too. In the bathroom by the lunchroom, the one someone had dubbed the "vomitorium." Once Marquez had been in there, plugging her nose at the putrid smell, when Dana Berglund had emerged from a stall, primly dabbing her mouth with a piece of toilet paper, her eyes wet. She'd smoothed her cheerleader skirt and checked her blush in the mirror. Noting Marquez's rolled eyes, she'd defiantly declared, "Everybody does it," before slipping out the door.

And there'd been that anorexic girl Marquez's junior year. Marquez hadn't known her. She was a senior, very popular, a 4.0, pretty. Real thin, but she always wore big sweaters, flowing skirts. One day she'd just stopped coming to school. Rumors floated around: she had AIDS, she'd taken a job as a roadie with a band from Miami, she'd run off to have a baby. Marquez heard later that she'd died. Starved to death. She hadn't known that was even possible.

She put the magazine down and went back to the ED door. With her ear to the glass, she could make out the faint noise of a girl sobbing.

She'd promised Diver she'd try this once. Summer too.

Marquez turned away. Diver had vanished and Summer had moved out.

She didn't owe them anything.

"Eighty-six the pecan pie," Blythe whispered to Austin. They were standing behind the coffee bar at Jitters. The café was quiet, but the lunch rush wasn't due to start for another half hour. "That guy on table five just noticed one of the pecans moving. Turns out it wasn't a pecan."

"The Roach War begins anew. This building's crawling with 'em." Austin sipped at his cup of coffee, his third this morning. He'd been up late with Marquez, then too buzzed with manic energy to go to sleep after seeing Summer. He was still buzzed, but it was solely the caffeine keeping his eyelids up.

"In my apartment I've learned to accommodate them," he said. "I split my food fifty-fifty, let them use the TV remote when I'm at work. I'm teaching some of the brighter roaches to play poker. The other day I lost forty bucks and a half a bag of Doritos."

"In my apartment," Blythe said, "I drown them in Raid. That works too." She paused to artistically arrange sugar packets in a bowl. "Caroline just pulverizes them with her foot. I'm really glad she's decided to stay a while longer."

Austin smiled. He liked Blythe, a pretty African-American girl with an easy smile and an open manner. She was fun to work with, and she never shirked on the side work, like some of his fellow waitrons.

He glanced over at the corner booth, where Caroline was reading a book and sipping tea. "You and Caroline go way back, huh?" he said, wiping down the counter. "Camp counselors. Very wholesome."

"Yep. During high school, at this summer camp in Virginia. That's how we met." She paused, sighing. "She's changed a little."

"How?" Austin asked casually.

"Oh, you know." Blythe shrugged. "Just . . . we used to laugh so hard, we were constantly snorting milk out of our noses. Now she's going to this really snooty college. She joined this sorority, and she's not nearly so down-to-earth anymore. Like, I mean, she actually *cares* about the difference between a Mercedes and a Lexus, Austin. Her dad's a small-town lawyer and her mom manages this clothing store, but they're not rich or anything, and all of a sudden Caroline's so money obsessed." She sighed again. "It's kind of depressing when people change like that."

Austin reached for a pot of hot water. "Speaking of, it's time for a refill. Maybe I can get her to snort tea through her nose. You know, for old times' sake."

Caroline smiled broadly as Austin approached her table. "You read my mind."

"I live to serve." Austin poured hot water into her teapot.

"Hey, you ever been to Crab Claw Key?"

"Sure. It's just down the road a ways."

"I thought I might go on a little shopping expedition. Coconut's not cutting it for me. It's nothing but glitter T-shirts and Speedo swimsuits. I'm looking for something a little more checkbook challenging. Saks, Nordstrom's, something like that. Heck, I'd settle for a Gap."

Austin laughed. "You want that, you need to head for Miami. Don't get me wrong. Crab Claw has some money. I mean, Senator Merrick used to live over there and Mallory Olan—you know, Diana's mom, the romance novelist—has a place. The main drag has a few nice stores, but nothing that fancy. We're just simple ol' folk here in the Keys."

"You're teasing me," Caroline said, turning up the volume on the accent. She pushed her book aside. "Besides, you're a guy. What do you know about shopping? I tried Blythe, but she's shopping impaired. I ought to ask Summer or Marquez." She paused. "Is Marquez working today?"

"She's coming in later." Austin poured Caroline some fresh tea. "I think she's a little distracted, what with Diver gone and all."

Caroline studied her cup. "Gone?" she repeated.

"Yeah. Just kind of vanished. But then, you know Diver. I hear you two are old friends."

"Where'd you hear that?"

"Summer. Diver told her you two got together yesterday to reminisce."

Caroline shrugged. She poured sugar into her cup and slowly stirred. The spoon shivered in her hand ever so slightly, but her face was a mask of calm. "We weren't exactly bosom buddies or anything. But yeah, we knew each other." She lowered her voice. "To be perfectly honest, he always was a little, well, odd. It doesn't surprise me one whit that he's run off like this. Does anyone have a clue where he went?"

"Nope. He didn't leave a note or anything. Very weird. We thought about calling the police—"

"Oh, I wouldn't do that," Caroline said quickly. "I mean, for one thing, they wouldn't do anything, anyway. I doubt he'd qualify as a missing person for a while. He's over eighteen, he has a habit of acting strangely. And besides, they're busy catching *real* criminals—rapists and burglars and murderers. . . ."

"No one said anything about Diver being a criminal. Real or otherwise."

"No, of course not," Caroline said. "I just meant it would be a waste of time to bother the police. I'm sure Diver will turn up." She offered up another broad smile. "So. When do you get off?"

"Me? My work is never done."

"Your shift has to end eventually." She brushed her hair behind her ear, an innocent gesture that nonetheless seemed scripted. "I thought maybe you might want to give me a tour."

"A most tempting offer. But I do most of my shopping at 7-Eleven. That includes my wardrobe and most of my home furnishings."

"Well, the offer stands," Caroline said, eyes sweeping Austin from head to toe.

Austin gave his best aw-shucks grin and headed over to a nearby table to clear away some plates. Caroline returned to her reading.

She was undeniably a very attractive girl. Too bad he had the sneaking suspicion she was also very bad news.

9

Seek and Hide

Caroline browsed a rack of bathing suits without much enthusiasm. The shops on Main Street in Crab Claw Key were having a sidewalk sale. Nothing special. Certainly nothing worth suffering over in this ninety-degree temperature. The cement shimmered with heat like nothing she'd ever felt before. Even in her tank top and shorts, she was wilting fast. She had a new pair of sunglasses on, the kind all the girls at Tri-Delt were wearing, but even with the deep green lenses, she had to squint.

She moved on to a shoe shop, sorting through a pile of leather sandals. No luck. Which was probably just as well, since she was going to be short on cash soon. Unless she could con her dad into sending her another care package with a nice fat check in it, she might actually have to consider getting a job one of these days.

But it wasn't this summer that worried her as much as next fall. Nobody knew better than she did that she'd squeezed into her sorority because her mom and her grandmother had also been members. She had the birthright. She just didn't have the car, the understated gold jewelry, the ski vacations at Vail. At the sorority house, a grand, crumbling structure on the outskirts of campus, she was merely tolerated, like a stray cat no one had the heart to kick out.

Visiting Blythe down here in the Keys had seemed like a welcome respite from the stresses of college. She was so mellow and uncomplicated compared to Caroline's friends at school. Being around Blythe had made Caroline start to think maybe she'd just quit the sorority and move into a dorm. It would be a humiliating social defeat, but a survivable one.

And then she'd run into Diver.

"Need any help?"

Caroline looked up, startled. A guy with a nose ring was leaning against the doorjamb. He had the spun gold hair of someone who lived from dawn to dusk in the Florida sun. Like Diver's hair.

"No, I'm just browsing," Caroline said.

"That's cool. Give a yell if you need

anything. The Aerosole shoes are fifteen percent off."

"Is there anywhere around here I could get a soda?"

"The Sandcastle, down the street. It's like right on top of the beach."

Caroline headed down the street toward the wide ribbon of white sand filled with sunbathers. She took a seat under a striped red awning that shaded an outdoor café and ordered a large lemonade.

She watched two guys in swim trunks pass by, surfboards under their arms. One paused, pushed down his shades to check her out, grinned, and moved on. He too looked a little like Diver. How would she ever track Diver down now? He was like all these guys, a beach bum, a nomad. He could be anywhere.

She sipped at her lemonade, then rubbed the damp glass over her forehead. She'd moved too fast, pushed too hard. She'd been so excited about her little blackmail scheme that she'd forgotten not to overplay her hand.

Without Diver she had nothing. With him she could have a nice little bundle of cash. She could buy the car, the clothes, the jewelry she needed to redeem herself.

Yesterday she'd been sure she'd had him hooked too. Something about the way he'd reacted to the talk of his father's death had made her wonder if Diver didn't really think he *had* committed murder. When she'd offered to tell the cops a nice little made-up story about how she'd watched from her bedroom window as her neighbor—Diver—had bravely tried to save his daddy, she could tell Diver had no memory of what had happened that night. The guilt in his eyes, the resigned, desperate sound of his voice, told her he wanted to believe her story, but he didn't.

Funny, when you thought about it. Because the little made-up story just happened to be true.

Of course, the police had other ideas. They assumed Diver had torched his house to kill his abusive father and then run. But she could clear him of all that. And there'd be plenty of insurance money waiting for the picking.

She opened her wallet to leave money for the lemonade. All her friends had a Gold Card and fat checking accounts. She could have them too, if she could just track down Diver and get him to go along with her plan.

She'd offered him an eighty-twenty split on the insurance money. Maybe she should have been a little more generous. Of course, she was new to blackmailing. And it wasn't like there were how-to books available.

The surfboard guys returned, ogling her again.

They weren't her type—no future, no cash.

Once upon a time she'd had a wild crush on Diver. Maybe she should go fifty-fifty with him. Then he'd have money to go with his looks.

First, of course, she had to find him.

Diver skirted the shore of Crab Claw Bay, keeping an eye out for anybody who might ask the wrong questions. Fortunately most of the expensive homes along the water seemed deserted. They probably were. These were vacation homes for the rich, and most people found south Florida in the summer way too hot for vacationing.

Diana's mom, Mallory Olan, was an exception. She lived here year-round, although she was often away, visiting friends in Europe or, like now, on extended book tours. Her huge house, a strange jumble of arched windows and fantastic turrets, stood across the bay from the Merrick estate. But Diana's house wasn't Diver's destination. Not exactly.

Pausing under a palm tree, Diver surveyed the area up ahead. It was quiet and still, as if the world had been stunned into silence by the thick, unending heat. He saw no one, no gardeners, nothing except his goal—the ancient stilt house on the edge of the Olans' property.

It was a homely, squat little bungalow, its white paint chipped and faded. From the center of the house a shaded stairway descended straight down to a small platform on the water. A rickety-looking wooden walkway ran a hundred feet from the grassy, shaded shore to the stilt house. The walkway wrapped around the house, forming a narrow deck lined with a railing.

Diver shaded his eyes, hoping to catch sight of his old friend Frank, a brown pelican. But Frank's usual spot on the corner of the railing was empty.

It was now or never. If Diver had timed it better, he might have done this under cover of darkness. But he'd had a hard time hitching back from Miami.

He could take the walkway out to the house, but that was more visibility than he wanted to risk. Hefting his backpack and sleeping bag onto his shoulder, he waded out into the warm water. When it reached his waist, he began to swim, doing his best to keep his stuff from getting soaked.

When he reached the platform under the stilt house, he hefted himself up. It was shady, if not cool. The tar-covered pilings surrounded him. The ripe, sweet smell of dead fish and saltwater filled him with a strange, melancholy joy.

He climbed up the damp wooden stairs. The

trapdoor in the floorboards was open. When it came to the stilt house, the Olans had never been much for security. Diana had told him that her mother would have torn it down long ago except that as a home to bootleggers in the twenties, it was considered a historic landmark, and she got tax breaks for keeping it more or less preserved.

Diver kept low, just in case he could be seen moving past the windows. The mattress was covered with plastic. The sharp smell of mothballs hung in the air. A thin layer of white sand turned the wood floor to sandpaper on his bare feet. It was hot and musty and mildewy and dirty.

It was home.

After the fire he'd been on his own for a long time, moving from beach to beach aimlessly. But when he'd happened on the abandoned stilt house, he'd known it was the place for him. He'd slept on the roof and used the kitchen and bathroom when he needed it. And the Olans had been none the wiser. That was, until Summer had moved into the stilt house. She'd discovered him, and slowly, irrevocably, everything about his life had begun to change.

He opened the front door and sat down on the old wooden walkway, his back against the wall of the house. Out here, facing the ocean, he was safely blocked from anyone's view.

He wasn't sure why he'd come here. He should have moved on, headed north. He was probably much more vulnerable here, although it was remotely possible that hiding out in Crab Claw would actually give him the upper hand. Who would come looking for him here? They'd all assume he was halfway across the country by now, not secreted away in his old hangout.

Besides, he realized with a start, he'd dreamed of coming here. This was the house floating over the water. The house with the girl's hand beckoning.

Of course, there was no girl. Just Diver, all alone.

He closed his eyes. The sun scorched his lids. The water licked at the pilings. He had never been so lonely. Even after the fire. It hurt so much more now because he'd lost so much more.

The air stirred. He opened his eyes. A pelican sat perched on the railing, his huge beak tucked under his wing. He blinked at Diver doubtfully.

"Frank," Diver whispered.

Frank tilted his head, ever dignified, then dropped a load of white poop onto the deck.

Diver laughed. The laughter kept coming, deeper and edgier, until it turned to sobs.

10

Life and Other Games of Strategy

"Checkmate."

Summer winced, her hand poised over a black knight. "That's, like, really bad, huh?"

Jared gave a slight, stiff nod. "That's, like, really dead. But you were fantastic, for your first lesson."

"You could have at least shown me a little mercy."

"Did you show me any mercy when we played five hands of gin?"

Summer grinned. "You're just lucky we weren't playing for cash or I'd have bankrupted you."

Jared leaned forward a bit in his wheelchair. "I prefer playing with you," he confided in a barely audible whisper. "Juanita always lets me win. She thinks I need the morale boost."

A rustle in the doorway made Summer turn around. Juanita was there, arms crossed, mouth pursed like she was sucking on a sour ball.

"Just tell me this. Is there anyone in the Keys you're *not* dating?" she inquired.

Jared smiled at Summer. "I'm pretty sure she's not talking to me."

"There's someone here to see you, Summer," Juanita said. "Again."

"Jeez, Juanita, I'm really sorry. Hardly anyone even knows I'm here—"

"It's okay, Summer," Jared interrupted. "Truth is, I'm beat."

"No wonder," Juanita said. "It's two-thirty, and you were due for your nap at one." She cast Summer a sidelong glance. "I'll take over here, Summer. Maybe we should consider setting a quota on your gentleman callers."

When Summer opened the front door, she found Austin sitting on the lawn, leaning against a palm tree and chewing on a blade of grass.

"Nice digs," he commented. "Even better in daylight." He patted the grass. "Take a load off."

Summer closed the door. "Why are you here?"

"I'm not here to seduce you." He paused. "Unless you're putting in a request."

"I'm working. And I've been informed I'm not supposed to have 'gentleman callers.'"

"*A,* I'm no gentleman. And *B,* it's about Diver."

Summer rushed over. "Did you hear from him?"

"No, nothing like that. Actually, this has to do with Caroline."

Summer gestured toward the palm-lined street. "Come on. I don't want to upset Jared. It's hard for him to see normal kids his own age. Not, incidentally, that you qualify."

They fell into step down the quiet street of manicured lawns, each one boasting tropical blooms in vivid pinks, oranges, and yellows. "So," Summer said, "what about Caroline?"

"Caroline was at Jitters this morning, and when I told her about Diver running off, something about the way she reacted didn't sit right with me."

"What do you mean?"

"She was just a little too interested in his disappearance. And her teaspoon was shaking."

Summer couldn't help smiling a little. "Her *spoon* was shaking?"

"You had to be there." Austin shrugged. "I know it's not much to go on, but since we know she saw Diver yesterday, she's our only lead. I thought about saying something to Marquez, but she's all worked up about Caroline as the other woman, and I didn't want to set her off."

"So what exactly do I do with this information?" Summer asked as they turned the corner. A stretch of palms provided spiky shade, but no relief from the sizzling heat. Beyond a stately white home the ocean sparkled endlessly.

"I'm not sure. I know it's not much. But I tried."

"You could have just called, you know."

Austin stopped walking. A self-conscious smile tugged at the corners of his mouth. "There may actually have been another reason that I stopped by. I may have wanted to ask you something."

His words had taken on a different tone. Summer knew it very well, that whispery and insistent way his voice got, like the sound of a river moving.

"I think we've kind of said all the things we can say, Austin."

He moved a little closer. She refused to look at his face, with all its complicating charms.

"I'm sorry about Seth and Diana, Summer," Austin said. "You deserve better."

"Thanks."

"I know the rules here. I'm supposed to allow you to heal, maybe have a couple rebound boyfriends, then come back into play. But I've never been much of a Miss Manners kind of guy. And besides, there are extenuating circumstances."

"Meaning?"

"Meaning you just dumped me. And as a recent dumpee, I don't think I'm up to waiting around. So I guess what I'm asking is, where does this leave us?"

She watched the bands of frothy white appear far out in the water, then vanish. "I don't know, Austin," Summer whispered. "I don't know anything anymore. I thought I'd made the right decision about Seth."

"Well, as you may recall, I offered a dissenting opinion on that one."

"If I could have been so wrong about him, how can I know anything?"

Austin took her hands in his. "Do you remember what I told you when you were trying to decide about whether to reapply to Carlson?"

Summer watched his fingers tangle in her own, trying to stay neutral, trying not to feel the feelings tangle up inside her in response to his touch. "Something along the lines of, 'Don't crap out on it just because you're afraid of failing.'"

"I'm sure it was much more eloquently phrased. Anyway, you see my point?"

Summer shook her head. "I need to go, Austin," she said, trying to pull away.

"My point is, I'm just another Carlson. You did the noble thing. You stuck with old Seth, who turned out not to be Old Faithful. But that was just a diversionary tactic to keep you from dealing with your feelings for me. So I'm giving you one last chance to claim your prize. It's the choice of a lifetime, Summer. Don't blow it again."

Summer smiled. "The choice of a lifetime, huh?"

"And don't smile all-knowingly like that. You know it's true. Besides, I find it incredibly sexy."

Without warning, Austin bent down and kissed her. The scorching sun and the heat of his body, pressed close to hers, made it seem like much more than a kiss, made it seem almost dangerous.

When he pulled away, a troubled expression had replaced Austin's confidence. "This is harder for me than you know, Summer," he whispered. "I'm not sure it's fair for me to try again like this. There are things about me . . . I don't know. I'm just saying I'm maybe not the best choice for you. I'm saying maybe I'm being selfish here. Hell, I know I'm being selfish—" His voice caught.

"I don't understand. What do you mean?"

"Nothing." He gave a helpless shrug. "Except, of course, what you already know. That I love you."

She watched him walk away without another word. Even when he'd vanished from her sight, she could still feel his fingers wrapped in hers, and she could still taste his kiss.

Austin walked home the long way, taking his time to skirt one of the less crowded beaches. He took off his shoes and let the waves cool his feet. The sun melted into his shoulders, turning the waves to dazzling prisms. "The always wind-obeying deep," Austin mumbled. That's what Shakespeare had called it.

Austin smiled in spite of himself. Here he was strolling down a Florida beach—a lost, lovesick, poorly-groomed poet muttering Shakespeare at the waves. What would his brother say?

He hadn't talked to his brother in a while. The messages kept accumulating on Austin's machine. *I know what you're going through. It gets easier with time. Don't give up hope, man.* Variations on the theme of coping.

Not that Dave was coping all that well. But then, the knowledge that you were going to die early, in exactly the same slow, awful way your father was dying, was bound to wear you down. Dave's fiancée had dumped him, he'd contemplated suicide, he was drinking heavily.

Not that Austin was doing much better.

He was hardly one to preach to Summer about how to make hard choices. What the hell did he know about choices? All he knew was that the idea of being without Summer so filled with him fear that he couldn't let her go. He'd humiliated himself again and again, returning to her life, making his case like an overeager lawyer filing endless appeals.

Even though he knew the kindest thing, the right thing, was to let her go. She didn't deserve to watch him get sick and die. She didn't deserve any of it.

Of course, that assumed a long and happy relationship together first. But he did assume that, like he assumed the sun would rise tomorrow and the ocean would still be blue and *Baywatch* would still be on the air. He loved her that completely.

It could be years, decades, before he had any symptoms. There was research going on, things were always changing. Austin had told his brother that after Dave had gotten the news. Dave had told Austin the same thing when Austin had forced himself to find out the truth about his own future.

Austin paused to toss a shell far out into the ocean. He watched it get sucked deep into the sea without a sound. The wind-obeying deep.

He liked that. Wind obeying. If the sea couldn't fight the wind, how could he? Whatever Summer decided, that would be it. He'd said it before, but this time he *felt* it. No more pleading, no more humiliating pitches like a desperate ad man. He would blow with the wind, let things fall where they might.

There was no point in fighting fate. It was up to karma. The great cosmic game plan. It was up to secrets coded deep in his cells. It was up to the wind.

It was up to Summer.

11

Not Good Enough

Diana slapped the Cheerios box to the floor with a satisfying *whap*. "Gotcha," she muttered.

The door to the apartment opened. "Anybody call?" Marquez asked hopefully as she tossed her waitress apron onto the couch.

"Nope. Sorry. No word on Diver?"

"Nothing." Marquez dropped into a chair. "And not that you and I are speaking anymore, but why are you crawling around on the floor with a box of cereal?"

"Not that you and I are speaking anymore, but I've spent all afternoon in search of the elusive Moby-Roach. This building is such a dump. He kept me awake all night, scrabbling around on the floor."

"Sure it wasn't your conscience keeping you awake?"

Diana ignored the question. "He's trapped inside this box. Now I just need to get rid of him."

"Finally. A guy who's your type. You should have shopped other species a long time ago. If it doesn't work out with Moby, you might try a cobra. Or a rat. Maybe a weasel."

Diana stared wearily at the Cheerios box. She knew Marquez was spoiling for a fight, but she just wasn't up for it.

Seth had stopped by this morning to pick up a duffel bag he'd left behind. He'd spent last night at his grandfather's, he'd informed her. No, he was not going back to California anytime soon. No, he did not want to talk to Diana about Summer, or about anything else, for that matter.

Marquez tried again. "It took you a while, Diana, but I knew you'd realize Seth was out of your league."

"This isn't going to work, is it?" Diana asked softly. "Just the two of us here in this apartment, I mean. Without Summer here, it's like there's no buffer zone to keep us from killing each other."

"I'm up for it. Swords or pistols?"

"Maybe I should move. I could go back to my mom's."

Marquez fell silent. The sound of laughter coming from the pool area in the backyard drifted through the window. "I gotta go look for Diver with Summer," she said, jumping to her feet.

Diana felt her will to stay cool in front of Marquez slipping. She bit down on her lower lip until it stung. "Look, could we at least just stop the fighting? I'm not up for it right now."

"You should have thought of that before you ruined Summer's life."

Marquez disappeared into her bedroom. She emerged a few minutes later, wearing what Diana had come to think of as Marquez's uniform—baggy T-shirt, baggy jeans.

In the old days Diana had gotten great pleasure needling Marquez about her tacky, too bright, *I'm extremely available* clothes. No more.

Marquez grabbed her car keys and her purse. "If Diver calls, tell him . . . I don't know, just tell him to come home."

She was almost out the door when Diana asked, "How was the counseling?"

Marquez paused, hand on the doorknob. "Fine, great. I'm a new woman."

"You didn't go, did you?"

"Actually, I did."

"I saw a counselor for a while, did I ever tell you that? After all the stuff with Ross, with him trying to rape me. . . ."

Diana could feel Marquez's eyes on her. But she just plunged ahead, stringing one word after another, touching each one like beads on a rosary.

"I went to this counselor, Lori, this one who worked at the Dolphin Institute. She was already kind of a friend—I mean, I knew her, so it should have been easy. But I went to her office three times and sat in my car and cranked up the CD player. I just sat there. I couldn't go in."

"Diana, I need to go."

"It was like I was afraid if I started talking about the feelings, I'd just dissolve in them. Like, you know"—she smiled—"like the Wicked Witch of the West. Which you probably would agree is not a bad analogy."

"Diana." Marquez was less angry than mystified now. "Why *are* you telling me this?"

"You have to try to get help, Marquez. Because if you don't, it just kills you. You die a little bit at a time."

"I'm outta here." Marquez yanked open the door.

"I got to this point, this really low point, where I was sure I was going to kill myself. But then I thought about all the things Lori had taught me. You know, how strong I really was, how things would get better." She smiled a little. "And it turned out she was right. I got through it. And so can you."

"Damn it, Diana," Marquez cried. She slammed the door shut. "Damn it, Diana," she said more softly. "I don't need this right now."

Diana sighed. "I know where it's coming from, the dieting and stuff."

"How could you know? You've never had an excess ounce on your bod."

"It's not just about that," Diana said. "It's something else—it's like you have to clamp down and take control of your life. It's like there's just too much . . . stuff in your head, and you have to find a way to shut it out."

Marquez said nothing. But she was nodding slightly, looking away. "How could *you* know?" she said at last.

"There's this feeling. This feeling that you get that you're not . . ." She met Marquez's eyes. "Not good enough."

Marquez cocked her head. "What is with you? You're not, you know, cracking up, are you? I mean, this is not the most likely time to suddenly be baring your soul to me."

Diana shrugged. "You're right. Go ahead, go. I'm sorry. I'm sort of bummed out, and you were the nearest thing to a human being I had around."

Seconds passed. Neither girl spoke. "I gotta find Diver," Marquez said at last.

"I know."

"You're okay, right? I mean, not that I care,

but I don't want to come home and have to call the paramedics."

"Like Summer did with you?"

"I wasn't trying to kill myself, Diana. I was trying to improve the shape of my thighs. There's a slight but significant difference." Marquez opened the door. "Want me to dump the roach?"

"I'll do it. I don't have much else planned."

"Bye, then," Marquez said, but she still wasn't moving. She stared at Diana with a clouded, annoyed expression.

"You know the thing I always thought was really great about you, Marquez?" Diana said.

"My voluptuous figure."

"The way you actually believed you were the coolest person on earth."

"Yeah, well, it was an act, okay? Is that what you want to hear?"

"But we're all acting, one way or another. And if you practice the act long enough, you start believing it."

"Maybe."

"You need to start believing in yourself again, Marquez. Trust yourself that it's all going to be okay."

"The person I love most in the world just ran out on me. Forgive me if I'm not feeling all that much like the coolest person on the planet."

"This isn't about Diver." Diana sighed.

"This is about sitting in your car, afraid to go inside. Try the counseling. Please try it."

"You know, I'm not the one who just destroyed her cousin's life. Maybe you should take your own advice."

The door slammed shut. After a while Diana took the Cheerios box down to the backyard. She watched the ugly, fat bug vanish into the grass. It was not particularly satisfying.

Still, she realized with resignation, it was the closest she'd come in recent memory to helping anyone.

12

In Search of Diver and Other Babes

"I feel like we've searched every beach in the Keys." Summer sighed as she and Marquez trudged back to Marquez's old car. The air was rich with the smell of coconut oil and the salty tang of the ocean. It was afternoon, and so hot that most of the beaches were nearly deserted, which had made the search for Diver quicker than it might otherwise have been.

Summer eased onto the torn front seat, gingerly lowering her bare legs onto the superheated vinyl. "You sure you don't want me to drive?"

"Nah," Marquez said. "The only way I can take out my frustrations is with the gas pedal. By the way, have I mentioned this is really nice of you, dragging around with me like this? You sure it's okay with your job?"

"Jared was great about it. Although he did mention that my life reminded him of a soap opera."

"Guess it's better than telling you it reminds him of CNN."

"Or *ER*," Summer said. "So. We've done Turtle Beach, Smuggler's Beach, Las Palmas Cove, and most of Coral Island. What next?"

"Much farther and we'll end up in Key West." Marquez tapped out a nervous beat on the steering wheel. "Maybe it's time to call it quits. For today, anyway. Who knows, maybe he called."

"He might even be home by now," Summer suggested, trying her best to sound like she believed it.

Marquez looked at her hopefully. Her big dark eyes had shiny circles under them. She'd lost so much weight that her cheekbones and chin had taken on a strange sharpness. She didn't look like Marquez anymore, but more like one of those caricature sketches they did on the boardwalk in Crab Claw.

"Want to get something to eat?" Summer suggested.

"I'm not hungry." Marquez jammed the key in the ignition. "I ate before."

"Tell me some more about the counseling."

"I told you. It was okay, no biggie. Not like in TV movies. Pretty mellow."

"And you liked the counselor?"

"Yeah. She was okay, I guess. For a shrink."

"So you're going back for sure, right?"

Marquez gave her a *back off* look. Summer held up her hands. "Okay, okay. I'm being nosy. It's just that you're my best friend, Marquez. I want you to be okay."

"I'll be okay when I find Diver."

"I know. But in the meantime you have to take care of yourself."

Marquez closed her eyes. "God, Summer, why is he doing this? I thought . . . I thought he loved me."

"Diver loves you completely, Marquez. You know that."

"Uh-huh. You didn't see the way he was looking at Caroline at the beach party."

Summer recalled what Austin had told her about his encounter with Caroline that morning. "Whatever this is about," she said firmly, "it has nothing to do with how much he loves you."

"But why, then?"

"I don't know." Summer tried to keep her fury at her irresponsible, selfish brother out of her voice. There was no point in getting Marquez more worked up. "I guess we have to remember Diver's had a really messed-up life. He's so laid-back and calm, sometimes we forget all those problems have probably taken a toll on him."

"Yeah, well, now he's taking a toll on me."

"I know. I'm sorry."

Marquez clutched the wheel so tightly, her knuckles were white. "I thought I knew him. I thought I understood him. You know what I mean?"

"I do know. Too well."

"You're thinking about Seth."

Summer smiled grimly. "Trying not to, actually." She nudged Marquez. "Come on. Let's hit the road, crank this baby up to fifty."

"It starts shaking uncontrollably at forty-five."

Marquez pulled onto the two-lane road that skirted the beach. Summer watched two Jet Skis fly across the calm water. "Remember when we took the Olans' Jet Ski out for a spin and they ran out of gas and we thought we were going to drown?"

"It was your idea," Marquez said.

"Whoa. Reality check. That was so totally your idea!"

They fell silent, the hot wind whipping their hair into tornadoes. "Sometimes," Summer said at last, "I feel a lot older than I was last year. Not just a year. More like, I don't know, five years or ten."

"Five years." Marquez considered. "That would make you a college graduate. An official adult."

"Well, just older in some ways. It's like

everything got complicated. It went from black and white to shades of gray. Last summer I was worried about not ever having a boyfriend. Now I've had two loves and lost both of them. Last summer I had a brother who'd disappeared before I was even born. Now I have a brother who—"

"Who's disappeared all over again," Marquez finished for her.

Summer squinted at a sign up the road. "Hey, would you mind taking a little detour? Could we run by Carlson for a second?"

Marquez put on the blinker. "When do you think you'll hear from them?"

Summer shrugged. "I have no idea. I reapplied so late. They'll probably reject me for being so indecisive."

"It'd be so cool if you went. I'll be right down the road at FCU. You could move back into the apartment, maybe, and then—"

"Not with Diana," Summer said darkly.

Marquez glanced at her. "I understand why you had to move out, but do you have any idea what it's like for me living with her without you? It's like having a pet scorpion in the apartment. I can't ever let my guard down."

"Maybe this fall, when the lease is up, we could get something . . ." Summer let her voice trail off. "There's no point in planning on it. Carlson's a long shot."

"They thought you were good enough to accept the first time."

"It was probably a clerical error."

Marquez pulled into the manicured grounds of Carlson, down a winding avenue lined by huge palms. "Where to?"

Summer grinned. "Nowhere. I just wanted to fantasize for a minute."

"So you're walking across the campus and, let's see, some babe like Brad Pitt is carrying your Intro to Something Irrelevant textbook—"

"No, this fantasy is babe-free. I'm carrying my own book."

Marquez stopped the car in front of a string of low-slung brick buildings with a view of the ocean. The campus was nearly deserted. "Mind if I get out for a second?" Summer asked.

Marquez smiled. "Take your time. But I'd advise adding a guy to that fantasy."

Summer walked over to the nearest building and peered through one of the windows. Desks, blackboard, table. Nothing fancy. But Carlson was considered a fine college, one for motivated and tough-minded students. It was difficult. It was competitive. Staring at the empty desks, Summer felt a slight shiver of fear skate up her spine. Was she motivated enough? Tough enough? Smart enough?

All year she'd planned on going to the University of Wisconsin with her high-school friends—and, of course, with Seth. She'd applied to other schools, including Carlson, but when Summer was accepted to Carlson and Seth wasn't, that had sealed her decision to go to UW.

Until, that is, she'd visited the campus with Austin recently and decided to reapply.

It would mean going to a new school solo, no friends, no Seth. On her own, no backup. Of course, they probably wouldn't reaccept her, not at this late date. So there was no point in worrying about how absolutely terrified the idea of being all alone made her feel.

She walked back to the car. Marquez was leaning against the headrest. The Ramones were blaring on the radio.

They drove back through the beautiful, quiet grounds. Summer watched the brick buildings blur together.

"How was the fantasy?" Marquez asked.

"Kind of scary."

Marquez started the car. "Maybe it needed a babe."

"I don't know," Summer said softly. "Maybe so."

13

Word on the Street

When they got back to town, the main street that bisected Coconut Key was bathed in the rich, unreal colors of the late afternoon sun. "I guess you don't want to come home and say hi to Vampira?" Marquez asked.

Summer shook her head. "You guess right."

"You know, all your stuff's there. . . ."

"I'll come get it sometime when Diana's gone."

Marquez smiled sadly. "I'd offer to do it, but it would be like admitting you're not coming back. Why couldn't Diana just move out instead?" She snapped her fingers. "I could slip a little arsenic into her coffee. Think they'd bust me?"

"They'd probably bust me. I definitely have motive and opportunity."

At a red light Marquez gasped. "Summer. Duck. I mean now. Jerk alert at two o'clock."

"What?"

"Crap. He saw you. Seth is over at the bus station, waving like a maniac. What do I do? Ignore him?"

"I thought he was at his grandfather's in Crab Claw," Summer muttered.

Marquez groaned. "Two red lights in this one-horse town and we get trapped by one! He's coming. Don't freak."

Seth wove through the maze of cars. A moment later he was peering through Marquez's open window.

"The light's about to change, Seth," Marquez said. "Make it quick."

Summer stared straight ahead, her heart ricocheting around in her chest like a pinball.

"It's about Diver," Seth said, just as the light changed.

"What? Tell me, what?" Marquez cried.

"I—" Seth began, but his voice was drowned in a chorus of annoyed honks.

"Oh, just get in already, Seth," Summer said.

Seth leapt into the backseat and Marquez hit the accelerator. He glanced at Summer, then quickly looked away. "Just take me around the block. My car's parked at the station."

"How'd you know about Diver?" Summer asked.

"I left my backpack at your apartment," Seth said. "I went over to pick it up this morning and Diana told me."

"Would you *tell* us already?" Marquez cried. "What about Diver?"

"It's not so good, Marquez. I've been kind of looking out for him all day. Checking out his old haunts, that sort of thing. I went over to his job, but nobody knew anything. Anyway, as a last-ditch try, I checked the bus station. One of the ticket guys remembered Diver. He bought a one-way to Miami yesterday."

"Miami?" Marquez echoed in disbelief. "Miami?"

"I'm sorry, Marquez," Seth said. "I wish I had better news."

"Maybe he just took a ride to clear his head," Summer suggested, knowing how lame she sounded.

Marquez pulled into the Greyhound parking lot. She dropped her head onto the steering wheel.

"Well." Seth looked at Summer again, his expression half resigned, half hopeful. "Anyway. I'll let you know if I hear any more."

Marquez pulled herself upright. "Thanks, Seth. For trying. You're a good friend."

"Well, then." Seth put his hand on the door handle, but he didn't budge.

Summer studied her nails.

"Well, okay," Seth said. Slowly he got out of the car. He closed the door, then put his head through the back window. "Summer, have you thought anymore about . . . you know, what we talked about last night?"

Summer shook her head.

"Okay, then. Well. Okay."

"Seth," Marquez said with a sigh, "you're babbling."

"Oh. Yeah, okay. Well."

"Thanks again."

Marquez pulled away. "What did you talk about last night, anyway?"

"Take a guess."

"At least the men in your life are within walking distance," Marquez said. "Miami, Summer! Who knows where Diver is by now? He could be in Alaska. Well, okay, not Alaska. But somewhere equally not here."

"Maybe. But . . . I know this sounds crazy, Marquez, but I just have this feeling he's not so far away."

Marquez paused at a crosswalk to let two bare-chested guys in-line skate across. "You're just saying that."

"No, I'm not. It's this feeling." Summer noticed a petite blond girl on the far side of the street. She was gazing intently into a store window.

Caroline.

"Hey, drop me off here, why don't you?"

Summer said casually. "I kind of feel like walking."

"But why? I'll take you to Jared's."

"I need to clear my head after seeing Seth, you know?"

"I understand." Marquez nodded. "You going to be okay?"

"Yeah. How about you?"

"Me? I'm invincible," Marquez said softly. "Permanently single, but invincible."

"Not permanently." Summer opened the car door. "I'll call you. Eat something nice and fattening, okay?"

Summer dashed across the street. The blond girl had vanished into one of the shops. Now Summer wondered if it even was Caroline.

And what she was going to say if it *was* Caroline?

She peeked into three shops, open late like all the Main Street stores. Nothing.

Summer was almost ready to give up when she spotted Caroline in a bikini shop called Swim Jim's. Summer sauntered in and pretended to browse a rack of markdowns.

"Summer? Is that you?" Caroline rushed over. "I heard about Diver," she said, oozing sympathy. "You must be worried sick."

Summer nodded. "It's so strange, Caroline. I mean, I just had lunch with Diver. He told me about how he'd gotten together with you."

Caroline put her sunglasses back on. "Yes,

we had a nice little get-together. Talked about old times and all."

"When you were kids in . . . where was it? Virginia?"

"Uh-huh." Caroline turned to the rack of sale swimsuits. "So what do you figure happened?"

"Well, we're still trying to piece everything together. Did he say anything to you, by chance?"

"Me?" Caroline put her hand to her chest. "Lord, no. It's not like we were ever *close,* Summer." She grinned. "Guess I didn't see his potential back then."

Summer hesitated. She was getting nowhere. Probably because there was nowhere to go. "So you two were never, you know, an item? Childhood sweethearts or something?" she asked, trying to sound casual. "Between you and me, I thought maybe you were trying to rekindle an old flame."

"We were just *kids,* Summer. And back then Diver never paid me a bit of attention."

"How about now?"

"Now? Well, he's got Marquez, Summer. I wouldn't have a prayer." Caroline pulled out a red one-piece and held it up. "Too blah, right?" She returned it to the rack with a sigh. "No, it's not like that with Diver and me. I have a beau back in Virginia. Kyle. He's a junior at my college." She cleared her throat. "So, anyway. You're saying there are no clues about Diver?"

"Not really. He might have gone to Miami."

"Miami?" Caroline demanded. She moved to another rack. "I mean," she added more calmly, "why Miami?"

"I don't know. Someone thinks he caught a bus heading that way."

"Lord, I hope not. For your sake, I mean. And Marquez's."

Summer hesitated. "Well, I have to get going." She started for the door. "If you happen to hear anything about Diver, let me know, would you?"

"Of course." Caroline smiled sweetly. "I can't imagine why I would, but I'll keep my ears open. And my fingers crossed." She held up another suit. "How about this one? Thirty percent off. I'm positively broke, but it's my size."

"Nice," Summer said. "Well. I'm sure I'll see you around, Caroline. Say hi to Blythe."

Summer stepped into the still-hot street. She'd heard nothing to suggest that Caroline had anything to do with Diver's disappearance. And yet she couldn't quite shake the feeling that Austin might just have been onto something with his shaky-teaspoon theory.

14

Hiding Out

So, Diana thought as she sipped at her coffee, *this is dawn.* It was rather pretty, if you were into that sort of thing.

She sat in the breakfast room of her mother's huge, fanciful house. It reminded her of Sleeping Beauty's castle at Disney World, lots of color and curlicues and excess. Not unlike her mother, Mallory, actually.

Diana watched the sun slowly grow, reds spreading like a bruise. On the edge of the property the old stilt house took on a pink glow. A pelican, probably the one Summer and Diver insisted on calling Frank, sat on the railing, looking positively prehistoric.

She wondered if she should try to get some sleep. She'd come here in the middle of the night after lying awake and restless in the apartment, haunted by images of Seth and Summer. At last, in frustration, she'd jumped in her car and driven aimlessly along the highway skirting the ocean.

Why she'd ended up here, she didn't know. Mallory was away on a book tour. And it wasn't as if Diana had a lot of cozy, Hallmark memories of this place.

But she'd needed to clear her head. She hadn't realized how confused and unhappy she was until she'd tried to talk to Marquez yesterday. Attempting to give her advice had made Diana realize how utterly unqualified she was for the task. She had her own problems, plenty of them.

She was obsessed with the idea of calling Seth and begging for another chance, and repulsed by herself for wanting someone who so obviously didn't want her. And disturbing her every waking moment was the image of Summer—or the lack of her, anyway. Her clothes still in the closet, her half-made bed, her shampoo on the edge of the tub.

Diana dumped out the rest of her coffee. Maybe she'd try for a nap and then decide what to do. She didn't want to move back to Mallory's, but she obviously couldn't keep living with Marquez for much longer.

As she turned to leave the kitchen a flash of movement out the window made Diana pause.

Someone was climbing up the stairs under the stilt house. She saw dark, tan skin, a glimmer of golden blond hair, then nothing.

Diver. It had to be.

For a brief moment Diana considered letting him be. She understood wanting to be alone, and whatever was wrong in his life, she doubted she could help him, if her experience with Marquez was any indication.

An image came to her suddenly of Marquez, her thin body racked with sobs. Marquez, so not like the old Marquez anymore.

With a sigh Diana opened the sliding glass doors and crossed the wet grass in bare feet, tightening the belt on her mother's robe. She knew if Diver saw her he wouldn't try to run. There was nowhere to go. And she had a feeling some part of him might just want to be found.

Diver was on the deck, leaning against the railing. He nodded as if he'd been expecting her.

"Not the best hiding place, huh?" Diana said, joining him.

Diver smiled sadly, his eyes on the brightening sky.

"That is," Diana added, "if you're really hiding."

He turned to her. His dark blue eyes were sheened with tears. He was so beautiful, a not-quite-of-this-world beauty. It was hard to look at him without thinking of his sister, of her innocent gaze and shimmering prettiness.

"To tell you the truth, Diana," he said wearily, "I'm not sure what I'm doing. I thought I was running. But then I came full circle and ended up here. It's like gravity is pulling me back."

"I know the feeling. I had no intention of coming here either."

She draped her arm around him and he laid his head on her shoulder. His skin was cool and smelled of the ocean. He'd been out swimming, of course. Diver loved the water.

There was a time not so long ago—last summer, in fact—when Diver had held her just this way. She'd been worn down and desperate after all the problems with Ross and Adam. Diver hadn't said much. He'd just been there for her, quiet and kind, on a dark, warm, sad night.

"Is she okay?" Diver whispered.

Diana considered. "I'm not sure," she admitted. "I'm just not sure, Diver. Marquez wants to know why you left. She thinks it's her fault."

"Oh, man." Diver pulled away. "Oh, man, I was afraid of that. . . ."

"What did you expect, Diver?" Diana said gently. "You disappear without a trace, not even a note—"

"I wrote a note. I tore it up. It was crap. It was full of excuses, and there aren't any." He wiped a tear away with the back of his hand. "There aren't any."

Diana touched his arm. "I could say something to her. If you're not ready to deal with everything, I could at least pass her a message."

"You don't understand," Diver cried, startling her with his sudden rage. Frank flapped off in a huff. "I'm screwed. I can't go back. I've lost Marquez, lost Summer. I've lost everything."

A slow smile tugged at Diana's mouth. "What?" Diver demanded. "What? You think this is funny?"

"Diver, no, no. It's not that. It's just that I could be saying those exact same words."

"I don't get it."

"Seth and I, we were . . ." Suddenly she felt embarrassed. Diver was so sincere, so innocent in some ways. "We were together for a little while, and Summer found out. They broke up and Summer moved out of the apartment and now I'm public enemy number one." She shrugged. "With good reason, I suppose. I just can't get anything right. I hurt everyone I care about."

Diana waited for Diver's shocked response. But all he said was, "You've never hurt me, Diana. I know you're a good person."

She let the words sink in, holding on to them as long as she could. "You're a good person too, Diver. Whatever this is about, you have people who love you. We can find an answer."

"There is no answer. I screwed up, and now it's caught up with me."

"You sure you don't want to talk about it?"

He shook his head, jaw clamped shut.

"No matter how much you're afraid you've hurt Marquez and Summer, all they want is to have you back. If you explained—"

"Did you try explaining about Seth to Summer?"

She looked away. "That's different."

"Diana, you have to promise me something. Promise me you won't tell Marquez about this. It would just get her hopes up. And there isn't any hope."

Diana stared out at the horizon. Deep reds were bleeding into the ocean as the cloudless sky lost color. The day was going to be a scorcher.

Diver took her arm. "Promise me, Diana."

"I promise. If you promise me something."

He smiled, just a little. "Maybe."

"Promise me you won't ever say there isn't any hope again."

Diver didn't answer. He just gazed out at the placid, blue water, lost in his private sadness.

"Nice sunrise," he said at last.

15

To Err Is Human, to Forgive Is Extremely Difficult

"Could I speak to Summer Smith?"

"May I ask who's calling?" a man asked briskly.

Diana hesitated. If she told the truth, Summer might not come to the phone. "Just tell her it's Marquez."

"May I also ask if you have a timepiece at your disposal?"

"I'm sorry. I know it's really early."

"Indeed. One moment, please."

Diana twirled the phone cord around her finger. From her bedroom window she had a clear view of the stilt house.

She wondered how long Diver would stay before moving on. She wondered if she was making a terrible mistake, calling Summer.

"Marquez?" Summer's voice was filled with hope. "It's so early! Did you hear something about Diver?"

"Summer, it's not Marquez. It's me, Diana."

Silence.

"Don't hang up, Summer. Just hear me out."

"I have nothing to say to—"

"Summer, I know where Diver is."

"If this is some kind of cruel joke—"

Diana sighed. "I'm telling you the truth. He's hiding out at the stilt house."

"You *talked* to him?"

"Just now. Look, I don't know how much longer he'll be here, so you need to hurry."

Summer fell silent again. "I don't have any way to get over to Crab Claw," she said at last. "I'll call Marquez. Maybe she—"

"No," Diana interrupted. "You can't tell Marquez."

"Can't tell her?" Summer's voice rose in indignation. "What gives you the right—"

"I promised Diver, Summer. I told him I wouldn't tell Marquez, and he trusts me."

"That was his first mistake," Summer said bitterly.

"Listen, I had real doubts about calling you, but my gut tells me maybe you can get through to Diver." Diana drew in a deep breath. "I'll pick you up. I'll be there in ten minutes."

Summer hesitated. "Okay, then." She gave Diana directions. "I'll be ready. Diana?"

"Yeah?"

"Is he okay?"

"He's your brother, Summer. You'll have to decide that for yourself."

When Diana pulled into the wide drive, Summer was already waiting. A woman dressed in white was with her and a guy in a wheelchair. At least, Diana assumed it was a guy. It was hard to tell, with all the bandages.

Diana parked next to a large van. The side door was open, revealing a wheelchair lift.

Summer met her eyes warily. She had on a T-shirt and a pair of cutoffs, no makeup. Her hair was damp and a little tangled. Still, she looked beautiful. She was clearly Diver's sister.

And Seth's love.

"All set?" Diana asked. Her voice was off, shaking just slightly.

"Diana, this is Jared and his nurse, Juanita."

Diana nodded. "Nice to meet you. Summer, we need to hurry."

To Diana's surprise, Jared moved his wheelchair close to her window. He fixed his dark, intense gaze at her. "Hi, Diana," he said in a hoarse whisper.

"Hi," she said, feeling strangely uneasy.

"We should get going too," the nurse said.

"We've got a long drive ahead of us. Jared has a doctor's appointment at nine."

"I'll probably be back before you, Jared," Summer said as she climbed into Diana's car.

"See you," Jared said softly. Even as she pulled out of the driveway, Diana couldn't shake the feeling that he was watching her.

"Poor guy," she said. "How was he hurt?"

"Car accident." Summer sat beside her rigidly, one hand gripping the door handle as if she might bolt at any moment. "He was in Germany when it happened. He went over an embankment, like a two-hundred-foot drop. He nearly died."

"Where's his family?"

"In New England. They never visit. They just, you know, pay the bills."

The conversation ground to a halt. Diana drove faster than was strictly necessary. The warm wind ripped through the windows. She wondered whose job it was to break the awful silence.

They were almost to Mallory's before Diana finally spoke again. "I'm not sure I'm doing the right thing."

"It must be hard to know, what with not having a conscience."

Diana let it go. "The thing is, I think Diver needs to tell someone what's going on, and you're probably the only one he'll talk to. He feels so bad about himself. About hurting Marquez and you. But something's really tearing him up."

"He didn't say why he ran off?"

"No. He didn't say much of anything." Diana turned down her mother's street. "Except that he didn't have any excuse for what he'd done. And that he'd lost you and Marquez for good."

Diana paused. She felt the words working their way to the surface. She could almost taste them, bitter and unwelcome as tears.

"That's . . ." She pulled into the driveway. "That's sort of how I feel."

Summer opened the door. Her face was blank. There was nothing there—no forgiveness, not even any anger.

"Thank you for calling me about Diver," she said. She closed the door.

Diana watched her run across the green, still-dewy lawn. She put the car in reverse, then hesitated. After a moment she turned off the car and went inside the house to wait, although she wasn't quite sure for what.

16

Did He or Didn't He?
Only His Sister Knows for Sure. . . .

The front door of the stilt house was ajar. The smell of mildew and ocean and mothballs made Summer instantly nostalgic. This had been her first home away from home. While living here, she'd met Marquez and Seth and Adam.

And Diver.

Diver, who by some amazing convergence of fate and circumstance and the alignment of the planets and the Quick Pick lottery numbers, had turned out to be her brother.

He was in the bathroom, splashing water on his face. When he saw her reflection in the mirror, he seemed more resigned than surprised.

"Diana works fast," he said. "I knew I shouldn't have come back here. I don't know why I did."

"I do," Summer said. "It's home."

"You shouldn't have bothered coming. I was just about to leave."

Summer followed Diver onto the porch. Frank flapped over to join them as they sat on the sun-warmed planks.

"Where are you going?" Summer asked.

"North somewhere."

"That would be ironic, since you ran screaming from Minnesota like a bat out of hell."

"Not *that* far north."

Summer leaned back against the wall and closed her eyes to the sun's heat. "So what is it you're running from this time, Diver? Or should I say who? Last time it was Mom and Dad and me. So who is it this time? Marquez?"

"I love Marquez," he whispered.

"Well, you sure have an interesting way of showing it. How could you do this to her when she's so fragile?" She opened her eyes. Her brother sat beside her, head bent low, his long golden hair half obscuring his face. "How *could* you?" she demanded in a voice choked by rage.

Diver's shoulders jerked convulsively. His soft sobs were almost drowned by the steady rush and retreat of the waves.

Summer stared at him without pity. He was an illusion, not a real flesh-and-blood human being. Like a movie star, she realized. A blank, beautiful slate, an image without substance. He came into people's lives and let them believe and then, when they needed him most, he vanished. He'd done it to Summer, to her parents, to Marquez.

"She believed in you, Diver," Summer said.

Long minutes passed before Diver raised his head. His eyes were bloodshot. His face was damp with tears.

"I'm going to tell you something," he said. "Because I want you to explain it to Marquez. So she understands. So she knows I love her. I did something, something really bad, a long time ago. Back when I was with my other dad, the one who kidnapped me. I was just a kid. I mean, it was a long time ago, okay?"

Summer nodded. "Okay."

"And this . . . this bad thing finally caught up with me. So I had to leave."

"And that's it? That's supposed to make Marquez feel better?"

"I know," Diver said hopelessly. He went to the railing and gazed down at the water. "Forget it. There's nothing I can do."

"I have a brilliant idea. How about fighting back? How about confronting whatever this thing is? How about trusting that Marquez and I would stick by you?"

Diver looked at her doubtfully. "Would you? I wonder."

"Maybe if you told me what it was, maybe then—"

"I killed someone, Summer."

The waves kept coming, the sun kept shining, the breeze kept teasing the palms. But Summer was pretty sure that the world as she'd known it was suddenly forever changed.

"Maybe you didn't hear me," Diver said sharply. "I killed—"

"I heard you."

"Do you still want to tell Marquez? Are you still planning on holding my hand, sticking by me? You'd look nice in court, the loyal sister."

Summer stood. She held on to the wooden railing. It was warm from the sun, smooth and shiny from years of exposure to the wild storms that spun out of the ocean. That's how it was, here in the Keys. One hour it would be calm, a little too calm, and then suddenly the sky would open up and you'd wonder how the world could survive such a beating.

She turned to face him. "I don't believe it."

"Believe it. It's true. I even have a witness."

Summer crossed her arms over her chest. "Tell me."

"I can't. I've already told you too much."

"You're leaving, anyway. What do you care? It's not like I'm going to turn you in, Diver."

"No."

"If you don't tell me the details, I won't have

any way to make it okay with Marquez. If you do . . . well, I don't have to tell her everything, but I'll be able to sell your story. You know, to make her feel like it's not her fault you left."

Diver pursed his lips. His brow was creased, his blue eyes so dark, they could have been black. "Let's go inside."

"Who's going to hear us? Frank?"

Diver managed a grim smile. "He's never been able to keep a secret. Besides, he's always thought highly of me. I'd hate to disillusion him."

"Why not Frank? You've done it to everyone else."

They went back inside. Diver shut the door, and they sat at the wobbly Formica table.

"So?" Summer prompted.

Diver sucked in a deep breath. "I'll tell you the whole story. But you can't tell the details to Marquez. I don't want her thinking about me this way. Just . . . just tell her I got into some trouble. Deal?"

"All right."

"There was a fire," Diver said softly, almost as if he were reciting a story he knew by heart. "My mom had died of cancer, and it was just my dad and me then. He wasn't such a great dad."

"Well, duh, Diver. He kidnapped you, for starters," Summer said, almost exasperated.

"Sometimes you act as if your growing up was normal."

"It was, to me. I didn't know anything else, Summer. And it wasn't all bad." He shrugged. "So, anyway, he beat me up sometimes. Well, a lot, actually. And one night I just got so sick of it that I burned down the house and he died and then I ran away." He said it casually, as if he were reciting what he'd had for dinner last night. "I was on the streets for a long time. Living here and there, and then I found this place"—he waved his arm—"which was like a palace to me. And then you came. Which was like . . . like waking up from a nightmare, in a way."

Summer fingered a plastic place mat on the table. "Are you sure he died?"

"I'm sure."

"How can you be sure?"

"I saw the papers. They were after me for arson and murder."

"But assuming you did it—"

"I *did* do it."

"Assuming you did it," Summer persisted, "you were just a kid, Diver. It was self-defense."

"It was premeditated," Diver said calmly. "I wanted him dead."

Summer got a glass out of the cupboard. The water in the faucet was warm and tinny tasting. She drank slowly, considering. "So how did you burn down the house, exactly?"

"I don't remember. It was a long time ago. Mostly I just remember it in dreams. I think I blacked out at some point. I remember coming to on the lawn. It was dark, the grass was wet. The fire engines were coming. I could hear my dad . . . screaming."

"But you don't know how you started the fire."

Diver was staring at his hands, as if they held the answer. "No. But Caroline said they found—" He stopped cold.

"I had a feeling she was involved in this somehow."

"She was my next-door neighbor. She recognized me right away, that night Marquez was in the hospital and I ran into her. I denied it, but there was no point. She knew. She knew all the details. She said they found flammable liquid at the site. She knew the cops were after me. She knew everything."

"And?"

Diver sighed. "There was some insurance money, I guess. She said if I went back and claimed it, she'd make up this story about how she saw me try to save my dad. How she'd been just a kid, too freaked out by the whole thing to tell the police at the time."

"Let me guess. In return Caroline gets a piece of the insurance money?"

"Something like that." Diver gave a harsh

laugh. "She really believes people would buy her story about how I was a big hero, not a murderer. How I'd tried to save my dad, even though he beat the crap out of me almost every day of my life."

Summer put her glass in the sink. She didn't need this to be happening. Her life was plenty complicated already. She didn't need Diver's problems.

Truth was, she wasn't even sure she needed Diver. He'd disappointed her so many times. She didn't owe him.

She turned. Diver was looking out the window at Frank, smiling wistfully at the ugly pelican. Sometimes when he smiled that way, she could imagine Diver as a child, desperate and alone and yet still, against all logic, hopeful. Hoping that his life really was normal. That his parents really did love him.

She joined him at the window.

"I want you to promise me something, Diver. And I want you to mean it. This can't be like all your other promises. This can't just be something you say to make me go away."

Diver looked at her, waiting. Hoping.

"I want you to promise me that you'll stay put for two more days. Right here. No questions. I'll be sure you have some food. You just need to lie low and give me a chance to figure things out."

"There's nothing to figure out, Summer. It's like I told Diana—it's hopeless."

"Do you promise or not?" she demanded. "Yes or no?"

Diver gave a small nod. "I promise. Just don't . . . get yourself in any trouble because of me, okay? You don't owe me anything."

"You read my mind."

He stared back out the window. "It's funny. I have those dreams again and again, but I never let myself see the worst part. I see myself leaving my dad. I see him burning alive, for God's sake. But I never let myself see the"—he cleared his throat—"the . . . you know. The lighting of the match. I can't bear to know that's inside me, I guess. I wonder why that is?"

Summer went to the door. When she opened it, the clean, white light was blinding. "I'll tell you why," she said softly. "It's because you didn't do it, Diver."

17

The Plot Thickens . . .

"That was quick," Diana said as she opened the door. "I take it that it didn't go well with Diver?"

Summer almost smiled. Not unless having your brother confess to murder was good news.

"I need to talk to you," she said, stepping into the wide marble foyer.

Diana led her into the white-on-white living room, with its leather furniture and thick fake polar bear rugs. A spray of lilies graced the grand piano in the corner. Even when she was away, Summer's aunt insisted on having fresh flowers in the house.

Summer sat on the edge of a white leather podlike thing that only vaguely resembled a chair. Diana leaned against the piano, her hands on her hips. Her dark beauty was even more pronounced in the wintry living room. It was impossible to look at her without imagining Seth in her arms. Summer could almost understand it. Diana was exotic and difficult and elusive. She must have seemed like the ultimate challenge.

"Diver's in serious trouble, isn't he?" Diana asked.

Summer cleared her throat. She didn't trust Diana for a moment. Still, it wasn't like she had any choice in the matter. Diver was hiding out here, and Diana knew about it. And for what it was worth, Diana was the one who had called her about Diver.

"Diver needs to stay in the stilt house for a couple of days, maybe longer," Summer said carefully.

"He can stay as long as he wants."

"I'll need to bring him some food and blankets—"

"Done. This . . . trouble he's in. What are you going to do about it?"

"I don't have a clue. Try to find a way to set things right." Summer forced herself to meet Diana's eyes. "Diana, no one can know about this. Not even Marquez. No one."

"Diver's been a good friend. You can trust me." Diana gave a short laugh. "I know what you're thinking. Let me revise that. On this, at least, you can trust me."

"I don't have any choice, I guess."

"This is different. With Seth . . ." Diana shrugged. "I guess when I'm in love, I'm capable of doing just about anything to get what I want."

"Including lying about Austin and me? Setting me up and using my own engagement ring to do it? Flying all the way to California just to be with Seth and destroy what was left of our relationship?"

"Fine. Yes. I'm a witch, okay? But I was right about you and Austin. At least I'm a perceptive witch."

"Maybe they can put that on your tombstone. Loving daughter, caring friend, perceptive witch." Summer stood. "Look, I don't want to talk about Seth."

"What you don't want," Diana said, "is to believe that Seth might have felt something for me and I might have felt something for Seth. What you don't want, Summer, is to have to believe that you and I are alike."

"Alike! Please." Summer started for the door, but Diana moved to block her path.

"You wanted Austin enough to risk everything, even Seth," Diana said. "And I wanted Seth enough to risk everything. Even"—her voice cracked—"even my own cousin."

"I have to go, Diana."

"I guess it's too much to ever expect you'll

forgive me," Diana pressed on. "But you expected Seth to forgive you for all your little indiscretions with Austin."

"I ended it with Austin—" Summer began, but Diana's dubious look gave her pause. She took a deep breath. "I have to go, Diana. There's no point in discussing this. If you want to talk about your—your *relationship*—with Seth, why don't you give him a call?"

"Are you saying you're not going to try to reel him back in?"

Beneath the sarcastic tone, Summer could hear a touch of hope. She considered all the hurtful, cutting things she could say. But she was way too tired. "I know this may be hard for you to believe, but not everybody goes through their life with such absolute certainty about what they want. I'm not you, Diana. Thank God."

Their eyes locked. Finally Diana stepped away and let Summer through.

Summer was almost to the door when she paused. "There's something else I need to ask you," she said, barely forcing out the words. "Another favor."

Diana crossed her arms over her chest. "On the heels of just thanking the Almighty that you weren't cursed with being me?"

"Okay, so it's really bad timing."

"What do you want? You've got Seth. You've got the stilt house. You've got my vow of silence. How about my car? My firstborn? I've got an extra kidney I don't use much. . . ."

"Remember how you proved Ross attacked you?" Summer said suddenly.

Diana blinked in surprise. "Why do you ask?"

"Adam kept telling you no one would believe his brother did it, right?"

"He was telling the truth too. Ross was a senator's son. And the Merricks had money to burn." Diana smiled, not at Summer, but at some private satisfaction. "Of course, I got the last laugh, such as it was."

"You got Ross and Senator Merrick to confess, and you videotaped the whole thing."

Diana clucked her tongue. "A shame, the way the tabloids got hold of that tape."

"I want to borrow your camcorder."

"I'd lend it to you, really I would. But Mallory gave it to a friend of hers. She's having twins and taping it for posterity. Which is one film opening I'm personally not dying to see." She eyed Summer doubtfully. "Summer, you're not getting in over your head, are you?"

"I don't have a clue."

Diana went to the hallway closet and dug through a storage box. After a few seconds she held up a palm-size tape recorder. "You might want to check the batteries. Mallory dictates into it, and she always leaves the thing running. . . ."

"A tape recorder?"

Diana pressed it into Summer's hand. "I have no idea what you're up against, but it might come in handy."

"Thanks." Summer slipped the tape recorder into her purse. "Really. Thanks. This might just help."

"Sometimes it helps to be a perceptive witch."

Summer reached for the doorknob. "Where to?" Diana asked.

"I'll walk."

"Summer, you don't have a lot of time. Diver's probably not going to stay put much longer. And it's a long walk back to Coconut."

They walked to the car in silence. "So. Where to?" Diana asked again.

Summer thought. An idea was taking root in her mind, but she wasn't quite sure what to do with it.

"Back to Jared's?" Diana prompted.

"No." Summer hesitated. "To Austin's, if you don't mind."

Diana's look said she was not particularly surprised. "No," she said. "I don't mind at all."

"You shaved," Summer commented when Austin answered the door.

He grinned down at Summer's legs from behind the screen door. "The question is, can I safely say the same of you?"

Austin swung open the door. He was wearing

a pair of pathetically dilapidated jeans. No shirt.

"I know it's early. Sorry," Summer apologized, avoiding eye contact with anything visible between his neck and the edge of his jeans.

"I apologize for the chaos. Showering's as far as I've gotten with my rehab."

"You're feeling better?"

Austin slipped his arms around her waist. He smelled like soap. "You gave me hope yesterday."

"I . . ."

"Don't worry. It was nothing you said. It was what you didn't say. You didn't say 'get lost.'" He kissed her softly, a sweet breeze of a kiss, then pulled away, smiling. "Can I assume you're here to tell me you've made your choice? You can't live without me, you need me every waking—"

"Actually, Austin, I kind of need your apartment."

"Well, living together is a big step, but—"

"Just for an hour or two."

He planted his hands on his hips. "You're living at the Ritz and you want to borrow a room at Motel 6?"

"I can't use Jared's. And I can't use my old apartment because Marquez can't know about this."

"This?" Austin's smile faded. He cleared a spot on the couch. "Sit. What's this about, anyway? There must be something going on if

Diana, the Other Woman, is serving as your chauffeur."

"It's a long story."

"I can be late to work. They'd lose all respect for me if I actually showed up on time." He sat beside her. "Tell me. Maybe I can help."

"The thing is, I can't tell you much, Austin. This is my problem, and I have to figure it out myself. Even if I get it wrong." She shook her head. "And I've been getting plenty of things wrong lately."

Austin studied her carefully. He reached into his pocket. "Here's the key. I've got an extra. You say the word, I'll be sure not to be here. Just one thing. You're not having some sleazy tryst here with a brooding stranger, are you?"

Summer took the key. "Let's just put it this way," she said with a smile. "Fresh sheets would be nice."

Austin laughed. "I'm a guy, Summer. Refresh my memory. What exactly are sheets?"

Summer tucked the key into her purse. "I'll let you know when I need the apartment. And thanks."

Austin reached for her hand. "Whatever it is, Summer, trust your instincts. It'll be okay."

"I hope you're right," Summer said. "But the way things have been going lately, I have my doubts."

* * *

Diana drove back to Crab Claw Key, feeling both exhausted and too hyper to sleep. After dropping Summer off at Austin's, she hadn't been quite sure where to go next. Back to Mallory's? Back to the apartment and the inevitable cold shoulder from Marquez? In the end she decided it didn't really matter. Diana was scheduled to volunteer later today, so even if she tried to get some sleep, she wouldn't get much.

It occurred to her that it would be nice if she could talk Marquez into going along with her to the Institute. Maybe if she saw other people going to therapy—kids in much worse shape than Marquez—it might do some good.

Nice idea. Too bad she and Marquez were barely on speaking terms.

Diana cruised down Crab Claw's center, past white clapboard buildings decorated with sun-faded awnings. The corner bakery was doing a brisk early morning business. Even from the car Diana could smell the yeasty aroma of just-baked bread.

She paused at a four-way stop and hesitated. Coquina Street. Seth's grandfather lived just down the block.

Mariah Carey was wailing on the radio. Diana turned her off. She needed to concentrate. Mallory's house was straight ahead. Seth's grandfather's house—and potentially, Seth—was to the right.

To turn or not to turn? That was the question.

Behind her an ancient woman in a Cadillac honked.

Diana scowled at the rearview mirror. The woman honked again, more convincingly.

Diana turned.

She'd only gone a few yards when she saw Seth. His back was to her. He was mowing the tiny lawn with an old-fashioned push mower. No shirt, his broad tan back sheened with sweat.

This was insane. She didn't want him to catch her spying on him like some lovesick kid. She braked, thinking she could pull a U. But the street was narrow, and she knew she'd just draw more attention to herself, trying to turn around. Better to cruise on by and act like she hadn't even noticed him.

But just as she passed the neat white house Seth turned the mower toward the curb. He looked at her. She looked at him. She told her foot to keep pressing the accelerator. But because of some unexplainable freak accident of brain wiring, her foot braked instead, and she pulled over to the curb.

Seth wiped his forehead with the back of his arm. He was just a foot or two away, close enough, almost, to touch. She knew he was going to say something ugly. She knew he was going to make her feel even worse than she already did.

"You're up early," he said neutrally.

She tried to swallow, but her mouth was dry as sand. "I don't know why I'm here," she blurted.

Seth shrugged. "I don't know why I'm here either," he said. "My grandfather says I should go back to California, finish up the internship. He's really ragging on me to leave."

"He's probably right."

"Yeah. I know. I guess I'm just . . . I don't know. Hoping everything will still work out. Waiting to see how the story ends."

"Me too." She forced her mouth into a smile that almost hurt. "Unfortunately I think we're hoping for different endings."

Seth leaned close. She smelled the sharp, sweet smell of freshly cut grass. "Are you okay?" he asked softly.

"Like you care?"

He stepped back. "Forget it. Just . . . forget it."

Diana stared out the windshield, unable to look him in the eye. "Just tell me this, Seth. All those times we were together and you were holding me and telling me how much I meant to you and . . . was that all just a big act? *All* of it?"

"I think—" Seth paused. "I think it was the same thing for me that it was for you."

She forced herself to look at him. “For me it was real, Seth. Is that how it was for you?”

She didn’t wait to hear his answer. She knew he would just say something awful.

This time her foot had no problem locating the accelerator.

18

Fairy Tales and Other Lies

When Summer returned to Jared's, he and Juanita were still at the doctor's. Stan, the butler, had left a Post-it note on Summer's bedroom door informing her that her mother had called. Summer was to call home immediately.

As she dialed her mom from her bedroom phone, Summer's first thought was that someone had died. Her second thought was that somehow her mom had found out about Diver. Her third thought was that her mom had discovered that Summer had moved out of the apartment and into the home of a rich invalid.

Of course, there was always *D:* None of the above.

On standardized tests teachers always said to go with your first hunch.

"Why on earth did you move out and why on earth didn't you tell me?" her mom demanded as soon as Summer said hello.

So. It was *C.* No wonder she hadn't done better on her SATs. At least no one had croaked.

"It's sort of complicated, Mom." Summer went to the front window. The van was just pulling up. "I got this job as a companion to a guy who was hurt in an accident. It's a live-in position—"

"But you and Marquez and Diana were so excited about the apartment, hon."

"I know. But this is a lot more convenient." She attempted a laugh. "No commuting."

"Are you sure everything's okay?"

"Well, there is one thing. Seth and I . . . we kind of broke up."

"Oh, no. Oh, Summer, I'm really sorry. Are you sure it's, you know, over?"

"I don't know, Mom. I kind of think so."

Her mother sighed. "It's hard to admit, I know. I got the final divorce papers yesterday, but I still can't quite bring myself to say *divorced* without choking on the word."

Summer watched Juanita open the van door and slowly lower Jared's wheelchair to the driveway. She tried to let the word sink in. *Divorced.*

Her parents were divorced. That meant two houses at Christmas. Two new phone numbers to memorize. Two separate people, strangers living different lives. Strangers who just happened to be her parents.

"I'm really sorry, Mom," Summer said. "I just wish you'd given it more time. You were both so upset about Diver leaving and all that."

"This isn't about Diver, Summer. It's about your dad and me and the way we look at the world. We're just too, I don't know, too different."

"But you weren't different, not until Diver came back and all the fighting started."

"That was just the excuse we needed, Summer. And I hope your brother doesn't feel he's to blame. Have you seen him lately?"

"You know Diver." Summer hesitated. "Even if you see him, you can't really talk to him."

Her mother sighed again. "Well, anyway, I'm so sorry about Seth. You always seemed like such a fairy-tale couple. Of course, that's what people used to say about your dad and me."

They chatted for a few more minutes. When Summer hung up, she realized her hand hurt from clenching the phone so tightly.

Her mother really didn't seem to blame Diver for the divorce. Of course, she was a mother. Mothers weren't supposed to blame their kids for big things. Just little things, like driving them to an early grave.

Talking to Diver today, Summer had been struck by the way he'd talked about his past as if it made sense. As if it weren't some awful, crazy, unspeakable melodrama. There were so many people in his life he'd had to forgive. Why was it so easy for Diver?

Why was it so hard for her?

Still clutching the phone, Summer opened her bedroom door and went to the top of the stairs. Juanita and Jared were downstairs in the foyer, Juanita fussing, Jared joking.

How many people had Jared had to forgive? Where were his family and his friends now, when he most needed them?

"Summer?" Jared said in his soft voice. "You up for a walk in the garden?"

"Be right there, Jared," Summer said. "I just need to make a quick call."

Summer returned to her room. She dialed Blythe's number.

Caroline answered. "Summer!" she exclaimed. "Any word on Diver?"

"Well, that's why I'm calling, Caroline. I was hoping we could get together. Maybe early this afternoon sometime?"

Caroline paused for a beat. "Get together?"

"I have a proposition for you," Summer said. "Something I think will benefit both of us."

"I don't—"

"Benefit us *financially*. I think you should hear me out."

"Oh. Oh, I see."

"Why don't you meet me over at Austin's place around two?" Summer suggested. "You know where it is."

"Two," Caroline repeated. "I'll be there. I'm glad you called, Summer. I have the feeling we can work something out."

Summer hung up. Two would be good. Jared would be having physical therapy all afternoon. She'd call Austin and make sure he'd be out of the apartment. She'd meet Caroline there and then . . . well, she'd figure out that part out when she came to it.

She was sitting across from him in the gazebo, reading out loud, looking as radiant as she did in that photo he kept hidden away. If he closed his eyes, it could almost be last year and Summer could be his girlfriend again, not his paid companion. He could be whole again, not trapped in a wheelchair because on one dark, unhappy, drunken night, he'd driven himself over an embankment, hoping, just a little, that he might die.

If he closed his eyes, he could be Adam, Senator Merrick's son with the bright future ahead of him. Adam, Ross's loyal little brother.

Adam, Summer's boyfriend and maybe even her love.

"Jared?"

"Hmm?"

"Are you bored? I could read something else."

"No, no. It's great. But maybe we could just talk for a while."

"Sure." Summer set her book aside.

"Any word on your brother?"

"No, nothing." She shrugged. "But I'm sure he'll turn up."

"I thought maybe your cousin coming over this morning had something to do with Diver."

Summer looked a little uncomfortable. "No. Diana just wanted to talk."

"To make peace?" He knew he was prying, but he couldn't seem to stop himself.

"I suppose. It's hard to tell with Diana. She's very, you know, complicated."

Complicated. He couldn't help smiling a little. Oh, yes, Diana was complicated, all right. That had been very clear from the moment they'd started dating. How long had it been now? Two? Two and a half years?

"Do you think she's still in love with Seth?"

Summer hesitated.

"I'm sorry. It's none of my business. I mean, I hardly know you. It's just . . . I guess I've sort of been out of touch with that for a while. Dating and all."

"That's okay, Jared." Summer smiled. "It's no biggie. I was just wondering what the answer was. Yes, I'm pretty sure she's still in love with Seth. But you never know with Diana. Like I said, she's complicated."

Beautiful, complicated Diana. Maybe she hadn't always been so complicated. Maybe that night with Ross had changed her.

After all, it had changed everything else. It was the first time Adam had wished he wasn't a Merrick. And it was the only time he'd ever wanted to hurt his brother.

Diana had wanted to press charges, but of course, the Merrick clan had circled the wagons, threatening and cajoling and intimidating her. Family loyalty and all that.

It had destroyed Adam's relationship with Diana. It had nearly destroyed her. And a year later, when had Summer found out the truth about Ross, it had destroyed Adam's relationship with her too.

But in the end, Diana had found a way to get even. The revelation that a Merrick son had attempted rape had been bad enough. But the revelation that the senior Merrick had tried to cover it up had done the senator in. He'd resigned in disgrace.

Still, it hadn't taken him long to think about a comeback bid, running for governor in New Hampshire. And his son's drunken accident in

Germany wouldn't have helped his chances any.

He'd visited Adam in the hospital, full of good cheer. Would Adam mind recovering quietly in Florida, he'd wondered, away from the prying eyes of the press? Would he mind doing it under an assumed name, just for a while, mind you?

Naturally, Adam had said yes. Family loyalty and all that.

"Jared? You okay?"

"Sorry."

"You were like a million miles away."

"I was just reminiscing about some old friends."

"Anybody you want to talk about?"

"No. They're long gone."

She reached over and gently touched his good hand. "Maybe not forever."

"Maybe not," he said, but of course he knew better.

19

Dirty Laundry

"I have to admit I was surprised when you called me, Summer." Caroline settled demurely on Austin's couch. "You said you had a proposition?"

"It's about Diver." Summer sat on the chair she'd carefully situated right next to the couch. She glanced—subtly, she hoped—at the laundry basket by her feet. Tucked inside one of Austin's shirts was the tape recorder Diana had lent her.

Before Caroline's arrival, Summer had tested it out several times, talking at a normal tone of voice from various locations in the room. It had only picked up her voice when she was within a few feet, and even then the words had been muffled and hard to follow.

"So, have you found Diver?" Caroline asked hopefully.

Summer smiled. "Well, that sort of depends."

"Depends?"

"Diver told me all about you, Caroline. How you know about his . . . history. And how you want a piece of the insurance money in exchange for clearing his name."

Caroline stood up. "I don't think you have any idea what you're talking about," she said sharply, crossing her arms over her chest.

"No, no, wait," Summer said, hearing her voice rising. She cleared her throat. "Just listen for a second." She went to the window and made a point of shutting it, then returned to her seat. "I do know where Diver is, Caroline. And I'm willing to tell you, for a price."

Caroline narrowed her eyes. "What kind of price?"

"I want a piece of that money too."

Caroline stared at her in disbelief for what seemed like several hours. "Well, you certainly don't mince words, do you?" she finally said, allowing a faint smile. "And here I had you pegged as such a sweet little thing, Summer. I had no idea." Caroline clucked her tongue. "Your own brother. My, my."

Summer swallowed hard. She shrugged, trying her best to look casual. "There's no love lost between Diver and me. Besides, there's plenty of money to go around. The insurance money from his mom's death, plus there's got to be a big bundle coming from the fire. Split two ways or three, there's still plenty."

Caroline watched her suspiciously for another moment. Then she leaned forward. "So where is he?"

Summer cast another nervous glance at the laundry basket. "What?"

"Where *is* he?" Caroline said, louder this time.

"Not so fast," Summer said. "We need to talk percentages here. It seems to me, since I'm the one who's making this work, I should take half. You and Diver can split up the rest however you want—"

"Please! No way are you getting half the money!"

Caroline walked toward the kitchen, away from the laundry basket. She got a drink of water, then paused in the doorway.

Summer felt her heart banging around in her chest. It was too far. She hadn't tested the kitchen area, but she was certain the tape recorder wouldn't pick up anything from that distance.

"If we're going to discuss this, Caroline, let's do it in the living room," Summer said in a slightly choked voice. "Someone might hear. The kitchen window's open—"

"No, it isn't," Caroline said dismissively. She arched an eyebrow and locked onto Summer's gaze. "Look, Summer, if you think you can muscle your way in at this late date, you've got another think coming. This only works if I can convince the authorities that Diver's innocent."

Summer grabbed the laundry basket and slid down to the far end of the couch, closer to Caroline. She pulled out a wrinkled T-shirt and carefully began to fold it.

"How domestic," Caroline observed with a sneer. "I guess you and Austin are still an item after all, huh?"

"What? Oh, this. I told Austin I'd do his laundry in return for borrowing his place."

"Does he know about Diver?"

"Nobody knows. Not even Marquez."

"Good. You need to keep it that way." Caroline sipped at her water, considering. "Look, here's my best offer. I'll take sixty percent. You and Diver split the rest."

Summer pulled out another T-shirt, folding it on her lap. She didn't want to overplay her hand, and she knew she wasn't exactly Meryl Streep. When her senior class had performed *Hello, Dolly!* Summer had been cast as Crowd Member Number Seven.

"Diver owes me, Caroline," she said. "I just talked to my mom today. She and my dad got their final divorce papers. If it hadn't been for

Diver, well . . . they might still be together. You understand what I'm saying? I'm *owed.*"

Caroline pursed her lips. "Okay. We'll do it this way. Fifty to me. Forty to you. Ten to Diver. It's not like he has a lot of leverage, right?"

"Excellent point." Summer's voice sounded a little too eager. She cleared her throat again. "Okay, then. I can live with that."

Caroline joined Summer on the couch. The laundry basket sat between them. The little red light on the tape recorder glowed from under a shirt sleeve. Quickly Summer rearranged the clothes.

It suddenly occurred to her that it wasn't like she'd heard anything worth taping yet, anyway. Was this a total waste of time?

She wondered, in a searing flash of doubt, if she'd been wrong about Diver all along.

She reached for another piece of clothing. "You know, I do feel kind of funny about this," she said. "I mean, profiting off a man's horrible death."

Caroline tapped her fingers impatiently. "Somebody's got to take the money," she said. "It's just sitting there in some bank, getting dusty."

Summer sighed. "But I mean, Diver *killed* someone, Caroline. Don't you think he should pay for what he did?"

Caroline blinked in disbelief. "You don't actually think . . . oh, man, you *are* brutal! Summer, you poor demented fool, Diver didn't kill his daddy."

"He . . . didn't?"

"Please! Diver? Sweet little Diver, with those beautiful baby blues of his? That boy couldn't kill a mosquito." She grinned. "It's funny, though. When I told him I'd go to the cops and tell them how I saw him trying to save his daddy, I sort of got the feeling Diver thought it was a made-up story. He was listening to me like a kid who wanted to believe in Santa Claus, you know?"

"I don't think he remembers very much about the fire."

"Well, I guess not!" Caroline said. "Truth is, I saw that boy run back into the fire three, four times easy, trying to save his no-good daddy, lord knows why."

"But why didn't you say anything at the time?"

"I was just a kid, Summer. Like anyone would have listened to me?" Caroline shrugged. "I suppose the truth of it is, I'd always had this mad crush on Diver, and he'd pretty much always treated me like the dorky little girl next door. I didn't exactly feel like I owed him any favors, you know?"

"But they accused him of murder."

Caroline shifted uncomfortably. "Well, it wasn't like he stuck around. It didn't matter what I saw, one way or the other."

"How do you think the fire started, then?"

"They said something about finding flammable liquid at the scene, and Diver's daddy—I guess I really shouldn't call him that since, let's face it, he wasn't—he was always refinishing stuff out on the porch. Painting, that sort of thing." Caroline hesitated. "Our yard was right next to Diver's, and we'd had a big barbeque that night. After the fire happened, I heard my daddy talking to someone about how he hadn't put the coals out properly. It was windy that night. I suppose one thing led to another and . . . well, I guess it doesn't really matter now, does it? The point is, everybody just assumed Diver did it. He had plenty of motive, after all. His daddy beat the hell out of him practically every day. And after the fire Diver vanished. It made sense for everyone to blame him."

"I suppose it did, at that."

"So." Caroline glanced at Summer out of the corner of her eye. "Where are you going to spend all that nice green stuff?" She reached for a T-shirt from the laundry basket. "I guess the least I could do is help you fold—"

"Don't!" Summer cried, yanking the shirt away. "I mean, you know. There's underwear in there. Austin would kill me."

"You know, I *have* seen male unmentionables before." Caroline shook her head. "If I didn't know better, I'd say you were actually blushing, Summer! So, what are you going to do with your piece of the money? I'm thinking about buying a car."

Summer reached down and clicked off the tape recorder. "I'm sure I'll think of something."

20

A Visit to Flipper

"I really appreciate this," Diana said for what had to be the gazillionth time.

Marquez jerked her car into the left lane. "I believe you've already mentioned that."

"I don't know what's wrong with my Neon. It was fine this morning. But the transmission was making this weird noise. Sort of like when the vacuum cleaner sucked up your scrunchie the other day. Anyway, it's really nice of you—"

"Shut up already, Diana."

"I mean, I've never missed a day at the Institute. The kids get so they expect you to be there—"

"Look," Marquez interrupted. "I am not doing this to bond with you. I am only driving you there so I can have the apartment to myself.

I can spend a few minutes with you in the car or be stuck with you all day. Guess which one I chose?"

Diana rolled her eyes. "Okay, okay. At least let me pay you for the gas."

"Just tell me this. What part of 'shut up' don't you understand?"

Finally Diana seemed to get the message. They drove in silence for a while. After a few miles Marquez flipped on her blinker and turned down a long unpaved road bordered by sea grass and scrub pines.

Weird. The silence was almost worse than Diana's babbling.

"To tell you the truth," Marquez said, "I thought maybe you'd moved out when I got up this morning and saw you were gone."

"I just went driving around. I couldn't sleep." Diana held her wind-whipped hair back with one hand. "Maybe I should, though. Move out. If that's what you want."

"If you move out, I can't afford the apartment by myself. So no, I don't want you to leave. Purely for economic reasons."

"I'm touched."

Marquez braked for a huge blue heron, slowly crossing the sandy road like a dignified old man.

"So, what are your plans today?" Diana asked.

"Why do you care?"

"No reason. I just figured you'd probably given up on the Diver search. I mean, at this point you just kind of have to wait and see if he calls or turns up, right?"

"Yeah. So?"

"And you don't have to work till tonight, right?"

Marquez parked the car in front of the long, cedar-shingled Institute building. "What exactly is your point?" she demanded.

Diana reached for her purse. "Well, it occurred to me that I'm only going to be here an hour or two, and by the time you drive all the way home and then turn around and come back . . . maybe it would just be easier to stick around. There's a lobby with some magazines, or you could hang out here in the car. Or you could, you know, watch the dolphins and the kids. It's pretty interesting, actually."

Marquez checked her watch and did the math. Diana was right, of course. "*How* did I get roped into this?" she muttered. "You're rich—you could have just run out and bought a new Neon."

"So"—Diana swung open the car door—"want to come?"

"I'll wait in the car."

"But it's so hot. At least come inside. It's air-conditioned, more or less. And out by the dolphin tank there's a covered area with bleachers where the parents sit. That's pretty shady."

"I'll wait in the car," Marquez repeated, shooting Diana her laser-guided *get lost* look.

"Okay, okay. But if you change your mind—"

"I won't."

Diana looked as if Marquez had somehow disappointed her. "Well, okay. I'll try not to take too long."

Diana headed into the Institute. Marquez sighed. If Diana wanted somebody to watch her play the saint, she'd have to find another audience. Marquez wasn't buying.

She moved the car to the far end of the parking lot, where she could at least get a view of the beach. The big tank behind the Institute was partially visible, very large and crystal blue. A few adults in bathing suits roamed around. Diana was there, talking to another woman in a red tank suit. A handful of kids hovered near one end, towels draped around their shoulders.

Marquez cranked on the radio, flashed past some nice reggae-sounding tune, and locked it in. She lay back against the headrest and closed her eyes, but that was dangerous these days. Whenever she closed her eyes, she saw Diver. Not some blurry, half-formed picture, but *Diver,* complete and in spectacular Technicolor 3-D, fully animated. Maybe it was because she was an artist. He was almost as real to her in her imagination as he would have been if he'd been sitting here, right beside her.

The familiar, awful ache came back, a sharp heaviness deep in her chest. Why the hell had she said yes to Diana? She wanted to be home in the cool darkness of her bedroom, hiding under the sheets.

Waiting for the phone to ring.

Marquez turned off the car and wandered around the beach outside the Institute. She could hear the musical laughter of the kids, the soft, reassuring voices of the adults. Every now and then a huge splash interrupted the steady ebb and flow of the voices. The dolphins showing off, Marquez figured.

She wasn't sure what it was Diana did in there, exactly. She knew the kids came from troubled backgrounds or had emotional or physical problems. They played with the dolphins and that was supposed to help them, although Marquez couldn't quite see what a big slimy overgrown fish, even if it did look like Flipper, could accomplish.

She sat on the front steps of the Institute building for fifteen minutes or so until she realized she had to find a water fountain or she'd die of thirst.

The lobby of the building was small and unpretentious. A wide window allowed a view of the dolphin tank. Marquez located a drinking fountain, then wandered over to the window. Diana was in the pool at one end, holding a little girl in her arms while a dolphin swam circles around them.

Marquez took a seat by the window. At least there were some well-worn magazines to look at. Of course, they were all granola magazines, things like *Wildlife Conservation* and *National Geographic.* On the plus side, the only models in these magazines had four legs and way too much body hair.

The front door opened and a pretty girl about Marquez's age entered. She smiled at Marquez, took off her sunglasses, and went straight to the window. "She's having so much fun," she murmured. She glanced back at Marquez. "My sister. Stacy."

Marquez gave a vague nod to show she was not particularly interested.

"You waiting for someone?" the girl asked.

"Yeah. Not one of the kids. One of the . . . counselors." Somehow using that word to describe Diana was like calling a vicious Doberman "Benji."

"They're great," the girl said as she sat across from Marquez. She had large green eyes set in a heart-shaped face.

She was a little chubby, Marquez noted, but pretty nonetheless.

"That's Stacy with that dark-haired counselor. Diana, I think her name is."

Marquez watched as Diana lifted the girl she'd been swimming with out of the pool. The tiny girl was stooped over, emaciated. Her bathing suit hung slackly off a body that might have been made of twigs.

"What's wrong with her?" Marquez blurted. She cringed at her own bluntness. "I'm sorry. It's none of my business. She just looks so, you know, frail."

"She's anorexic," the girl said matter-of-factly. "You think this is bad, you should have seen her a couple of months ago. She's put on seventeen pounds since then. Coming here's helped a lot, I think. And she's seeing a therapist. She was in the hospital for nine weeks. We thought she was going to . . ." Her voice trailed off.

"But she's so young."

"Fifteen."

Marquez went to the window. That delicate, breakable, line drawing of a human being was only three years younger than she was?

"I hate to drag her away, but she's got a doctor's appointment," the girl said. "She loves coming here so much. It's funny"—she started for the door that led to the pool area—"we had to practically drag her here the first few times. She was so afraid."

Marquez watched through the window as the girl walked out to the pool, greeted Stacy, and helped her towel off. Diana helped Stacy put on a sweatsuit. It seemed ridiculous in the ninety-degree heat, but of course, Stacy was probably cold.

Marquez was cold a lot too.

It wasn't the same thing. She wasn't like that. She wasn't ever going to be like that.

Stacy, her sister, and Diana entered the lobby. Diana didn't seem entirely surprised to see Marquez. "Stace, this is my, um, my friend Marquez," Diana said.

Stacy smiled shyly. Her lips had a bluish cast. Her blond hair hung in wet ropes.

"Hi," Marquez said. "Looked like you were having a good time out there."

"I rode one of the dolphins."

"Yeah," Marquez said awkwardly, "I can see how that would be pretty cool."

"We're late already," Stacy's sister said, checking her watch. "See you next week, Diana."

Diana gave Stacy a hug. "Take care of yourself, promise?"

"Yep." Stacy glanced at Marquez. "See you," she said.

"Yeah," Marquez replied. "See you."

Diana wrung out her hair. "I'll just be a few more minutes."

Marquez nodded, watching as the door closed behind Stacy and her sister.

"Is she going to be okay?"

"I don't know. Maybe. She's tougher than she looks."

Diana returned to the pool area, and Marquez went back outside. The heat felt good on her face. She watched an old Honda circle the parking lot. It passed her on the way out.

Stacy was sitting on the passenger side. She was looking at Marquez. She waved, and Marquez waved back.

Stacy smiled as if they were old friends.

As if they shared a secret.

21

Reaching Out

For the third time Diver rewound the tape.

Summer stood next to him on the deck of the stilt house, waiting, hoping. Her face was flushed.

Diver fast-forwarded, then pushed the play button. Caroline's muffled laughter filled the air.

Truth is, I saw that boy run back into the fire three, four times easy, trying to save his no-good daddy, lord knows why.

Diver closed his eyes and he was there again, in that place the dream always made him go.

He could see himself running through the inferno. He could see his father lying under a burning support beam, his clothes on fire, his hair, his skin.

He could hear the screams.

Diver reached for his father's hand. He pulled, trying like he'd never tried for anything in his life.

There was nothing he could do. Nothing.

The sirens were coming. The fire was roaring like a thing alive.

There was nothing more Diver could do, except, just maybe, save himself.

He opened his eyes. The sun made diamonds of the waves.

In his dream there was always a hand, familiar and yet not, reaching out to him. There was always an old, rickety house, floating over a blue, endless ocean.

There was always hope.

Summer held out her hand. "It's going to be okay, Diver."

He took her hand, wiped away a tear, smiled a little. "You did all this for me. Why?"

"I don't know. I guess because it hurt to see you hurting." She shrugged. "And because you're my brother, Diver."

"I don't know what to do now."

"We'll go back to Virginia. We have the tape. We'll clear the whole mess up. Maybe Dad and Mom can meet us. It'll be fine. You'll see."

"I can't ask them to do that. Not after everything I've already put them through."

"What about all you've been through?"

Diver shrugged. "Not so much, really."

"I don't know . . ." Summer paused, frowning with concentration, as if she were searching for the very last word in a crossword puzzle. "I don't know if I'd be as kind as you are, Diver. If I'd gone through all you have, I mean. That's something I've had to realize this summer. I'm not very good at forgiving people. I sure haven't been very good at forgiving you."

He smiled. "Maybe I don't deserve it."

"Or maybe I needed someone to be mad at. Maybe I needed a reason for the divorce to have happened. That way, it kind of made sense. I didn't want to think that a relationship could just end for no reason."

Diver watched as Frank swooped past, searching for an afternoon snack. His life was so simple. Eat, sleep in the sun, survive. Sometimes Diver wished his life could be like that.

He looked at Summer, at his sister who'd loved him enough to help him. Enough to forgive him.

Sometimes he was glad his life was so complicated.

"I don't think relationships just end for no reason," Diver said. "Sometimes it's too complicated for us to understand. All these interconnected things have to be just right before you can have love. That's why it's so amazing when it happens. Maybe it shouldn't be so surprising when it doesn't last. Maybe we should just be astounded that it happens at all."

Summer nodded. "I'm sorry I blamed you for the divorce," she said. "I was wrong."

"I'm sorry I let you down."

"You didn't. I let myself down."

Summer laid her head on Diver's shoulder. They stared out at the water, bluer than the sky and just as endless. Frank scooped a fish into his massive beak and returned to the deck, preening and strutting just a bit to show he hadn't lost his touch.

Diver took a deep breath. "I'm afraid," he whispered. "I don't think I have the courage to go see her."

"Marquez loves you, Diver. All she wants is to have you back."

"But I ran out, I hurt her—"

"That doesn't matter. She'll understand." Summer grinned. "She's quicker at forgiving than I am."

Diver gave her a dubious look.

"Well, okay, she gets madder up front, but she gets over it faster." Summer pulled on his hand. "Come on. You can't hide here forever."

"No, I guess not."

They walked to Coconut Key together, savoring the sun, saying little. Diver tried to plan what he would say to Marquez, but he wasn't much for speeches, and besides, what could he really say except "I'm sorry"?

As if that would be enough.

When they climbed the stairs to the girls' apartment, his heart quickened. He grabbed Summer's arm. "I'm not ready. I can't, not yet."

"Diver, you have to. She needs you."

Before he could protest, Summer unlocked the door. Diana was lying on the couch. The TV was on. She sat up in surprise and clicked the remote control.

"Is Marquez here?" Summer asked.

"What happened?" Diana asked. "Diver, I thought you were at the stilt house—"

"It's okay," Diver said. "Summer worked things out. With a little help from your tape recorder."

"That's great news." Diana smiled. "Really great. Look, Marquez isn't here. I think she's scheduled to work tonight, though."

"Do you know where she is?" Summer asked.

"I don't think I'm supposed to know." Diana seemed uncomfortable. "I overheard her making a call when we got back from the Institute this afternoon. She was talking to the Eating Disorders Clinic at the hospital. I think maybe she went over there. I didn't want to push it by asking."

Summer looked at Diver. "You want

company? I'll walk you over to the hospital."

"I think I can take it from here," Diver said. He kissed Summer on the cheek. "Thank you. For everything. You too, Diana. I owe you both." He paused in the doorway. "It's too bad you two hate each other. You make a pretty great team."

He got off on the wrong floor at the hospital and took two wrong turns before he found the Eating Disorders Clinic. The waiting area was empty. Diver took a seat, thumbed through a worn *People,* paced awhile.

He was so proud of Marquez for coming here, especially in the middle of the mess he'd created. How was he ever going to tell her that?

The clinic door opened. He saw a girl, too thin, too beautiful.

Marquez. Her back was to him.

How was he ever going to make her believe she could trust him not to leave again?

She was nodding, talking to a woman who was smiling. "Okay, then. I'll see you next week," Marquez said.

How was he ever going to make her believe how much he needed her? What kind of words were there for that?

She turned. The door closed. She looked past him, then back. Her mouth formed the word: *Diver.* She ran to him.

He took her in his arms and held her till she felt like a part of him. She was sobbing softly, and so was he.

He kissed her, again and again and again.

"I love you," he whispered, and suddenly he realized he'd known what to say after all.

22

Diana Meets Up with Her Past, Summer Says Good-bye to Hers

The next afternoon Diana made her way down the winding garden path at the rear of Jared's home. Just as his nurse had said, Summer and Jared were sitting at the edge of the beach. Summer was on a bench, reading. Jared was in his wheelchair, staring out at the ocean.

Diana fingered the envelope from Carlson. Suddenly she regretted coming here. Yesterday, after all the stuff with Diver, it had almost seemed like she and Summer had reached a kind of uneasy truce. But if this was a rejection letter, Diana was going to look as if she'd come over to gloat.

Jared noticed her approaching even before Summer did. "Diana?" he said in that whispery, odd voice of his.

"I'm sorry to interrupt," Diana said.

Summer turned and took off her sunglasses. "What are you doing here? Is everything okay with Marquez and Diver?"

Diana laughed. "Are you kidding? I've barely seen them since Diver caught up with her at the hospital yesterday. This morning she was floating around the apartment like she was filled with helium." She held out the envelope. "This just came in the mail. I thought you might want to see it."

Summer took the envelope and read the return address. "It's too thin," she said flatly. "It's a rejection."

"They accepted you once, Summer," Diana pointed out. "If they reject you now, it's just because you reapplied too late and they were already full."

Summer stared warily at the envelope as if it contained plutonium.

"Well—" Diana took a step back. "I guess I should get going. Oh, we got the phone bill too. Your share's twenty-one bucks and some change." She smiled. "Good luck."

"Thanks for bringing this by," Summer said, not sounding altogether sure she meant it.

"Neither rain nor sleet nor heat nor gloom of night," Diana said. "See you, Jared."

"See you." He was gazing at her out of those penetrating dark eyes again. It was very unnerving.

"And Diana?" Summer said. "Thanks for helping with Diver."

"He means a lot to me too, Summer."

"Wait," Summer said. "You might as well stick around. You'll hear soon enough, one way or the other." She tore open the envelope. "Here goes nothing."

She pulled out the letter and scanned to the bottom. "Idiots," she muttered darkly. Suddenly she broke into a huge grin. "They're actually letting me in!"

"Congratulations, Summer," Diana said.

"Way to go." Jared held out his hand and Summer clasped it in both of hers.

"I can't believe it," Summer said, glowing. "I really can't believe it." She passed the letter to Jared. "Read it, okay? To be sure I'm not hallucinating."

Diana started to leave, then hesitated. She should have been thinking about other things, about how this meant Summer was staying in the Keys, or how upset Seth was going to be when he heard the news.

But something else was troubling her. Jared was holding Summer's acceptance letter in his uninjured hand. A heavy gold ring glittered on his finger, a lion's head carved onto either side of a deep blue stone.

There was something familiar about that ring. It was very striking. Expensive, unique.

She'd seen a ring like that once before. On the finger of Adam's brother, Ross.

Summer looked over at her. "You okay, Diana? You look like you just saw a ghost."

"Something like that," Diana said softly as she started down the path.

The Carlson campus was quiet, softened by late afternoon shadows. Summer walked the grounds, taking in trees and statues and buildings as if she owned each and every one. The initial high of being reaccepted had worn off, replaced by a tingling, edgy nervousness that was part anticipation, part dread.

It was like diving into a lake without knowing how deep it was. Sure, the admissions people had decided she could handle this school. Her high-school teachers had told her she could handle it. But part of her was still convinced she was being set up for an elaborate practical joke. She'd show up for class the first day, laden with heavy textbooks, only to have the entire college leap up in unison and yell, *"April Fools!"*

The University of Wisconsin, with all her friends—and with Seth—seemed like such a comforting choice now that she'd sealed her fate and decided against it. She would have felt secure there, safe. Here she was going to feel utterly and completely alone.

She went back to the car, which Marquez

had lent her, and waited for Seth. She'd asked him to meet her here. She wasn't sure why. It seemed like the right place to say what she had to say.

A few minutes later he parked alongside her, smiling shyly. She led him to a bench beside a shimmering fountain.

"So," he said, "everything's going to be okay with Diver?"

"I think so. I talked to my dad last night and he's making some calls. And Diver called me right before I drove over here. He confronted Caroline today with that tape I made. I don't exactly know what he said to her. But I do know I haven't heard him laugh so much in a long time."

Seth dipped his hand in the fountain pool. "That's cool. I'm really glad. Diver's a good guy. Man, he's been through a lot."

Summer nodded. The fountain whispered, filling the air with the musical sound of first rain.

"I was wondering why you wanted to meet here," Seth said. "But then it clicked. You got reaccepted, didn't you?"

"Yeah. I just got the letter."

"And you're definitely going to go here? UW's out of the picture?"

"I'm going to try it for a semester, anyway. I have to try, Seth, or I'll always regret it."

Seth nodded, his expression stony.

"It's like your internship, Seth. You really should go back to California, finish it up."

"I know. I guess I was just . . . waiting. In case."

"I've been thinking a lot about us. About all the mess this summer, Austin and Diana and you and me. I realized when I was trying to help Diver that I'm not very good at forgiving people. What happened between you and Diana, it really hurt me, and I couldn't see past that to the fact that I'd hurt you too. I couldn't forgive you any better than I could forgive Diver."

"There's plenty of guilt to go around," Seth said with a grim smile.

"I think I'm ready to forgive you, Seth. I think I can even start to forgive myself for messing things up so badly."

Seth reached for her hand. "Then you want to get back—"

"No," she said gently. "When I got past the anger and the forgiving, I realized something else. I've changed this summer, Seth. I've started to see how complicated life is. My parents divorcing. Diver's problems. You, Austin, Diana. All the stuff with Marquez. I mean, I thought all I'd do this summer was get some minimum wage job and perfect my tan. But it's ended up being a little more work than that."

"So what are you saying?" Seth tightened his grip on her fingers.

"I'm saying that if life's going to keep being so damn complicated, I want some time to get my head on straight. I want to concentrate on school. And on knowing I can count on myself to get through the tough stuff." She looked away, fighting tears. "I don't want to have to devote all my energy to trying to fix us, Seth. The truth is, I think we're past the point of fixing."

He released his grip. "Okay. Okay, then. I hear you."

"Diver said something to me, about how it's amazing love ever happens at all. Think about it. Two people have to get their brains and their hearts and . . . other elements of their anatomy . . . all in sync. And then the circumstances of their lives have to be in sync too." Summer sighed. "It seems to me we got the first part right, but the timing on that second part, the other stuff in our lives, isn't quite on track."

"This is because of Austin, isn't it?"

"I do love Austin, Seth. Just like I think some part of you, whether you'll admit or not, is in love with Diana. But that's not what this is about. It's not about Austin. It's about me. I know that seems selfish. But if I'm not sure of who I am and how strong I am, how can I ever really be someone you can trust and love?"

Seth kissed her, an achingly soft kiss that made her wish, for just a moment, that she could take back everything she'd said. "I'll always love you, Summer. And I'll always trust you. But I think I understand why you have to do this. Just be sure *you* understand one thing."

"What's that?"

"I will always be there for you. I don't care if I'm in Wisconsin and you're in the Keys. I don't care if I'm on Mars and you're on Venus. It doesn't matter. I'll always be there."

He touched Summer's cheek. He gave a small, sad smile. And then Seth walked out of her life forever.

23

The Pretenders

When Diana found him the next morning, he was in the bus station, duffel bag at his feet, dozing lightly.

"Seth," she said. She took the seat beside him.

He opened his eyes. "How'd you—"

"Summer told Marquez what went on between you two yesterday. I wormed it out of Marquez, then I called your grandfather this morning."

Seth rubbed his eyes. Outside, a Greyhound belched black smoke. A line of passengers was forming.

"I'm glad you're going back," Diana said. "It would have been a shame to blow off the internship."

He shrugged. "I didn't want the whole summer to be a loss. Although it sure hasn't turned out like I'd planned."

"Me either." Diana smiled. "Not even close."

"I thought about calling you to say goodbye. But I figured you'd take it the wrong way."

"The 'wrong way' being—?"

"You know. Summer dumps me, so I grab the nearest phone and call Bachelorette Number Two."

"Yeah, I have to admit that's pretty much how it would have looked."

"But that wasn't why I was going to call. I was going to say, you know, I was sorry. I think I pretty much treated you like crap, Diana."

"Well, I wasn't exactly a saint," she admitted. She cocked her head, smiling at him a little. "So what brought on this revelation?"

Seth shrugged. "I don't know. I guess I wasn't even really surprised yesterday. About Summer, I mean. I was holding out hope, but I kind of knew. And as I was sitting there, listening to her tell me it was over, I sort of flashed on how you must have felt this summer, hoping maybe you and I would . . . you know. Work things out."

"You've always been pretty straight with me, Seth. I knew the deal. I knew you were in love with Summer." Diana sighed. "I just didn't want to believe it. I wanted to pretend things were different. Sometimes it's more fun pretending than it is just letting go."

"Yeah." Seth nodded. "But it hurts worse when you finally do let go. It hurts like major hell."

Diana rose to her feet. "Well, I just wanted to say good-bye."

Seth slung his duffel bag over his shoulder. "I'll run into you one of these days, I'm sure. Maybe at Christmas, who knows?" He stood. "Maybe sooner."

Diana stared at the floor. She wanted to touch him one last time, but she knew it would just be one more awkward moment in a long string of them.

On the other hand, what did she have to lose? She'd already lost Seth.

Diana reached for him and hung on longer than she knew she should have. She put her lips to his ear.

The words were out before she had time to stop them.

"Did you even love me a little?" she whispered.

Instantly she was sorry. It was an awful, humiliating, desperate thing to say. She knew so much better.

She let go and turned away quickly so Seth wouldn't see her face. But he caught her arm and pulled her back to him.

"You know I did," he said, almost angrily. "Did *you?*"

Diana's breath caught.

Tell the truth.

If she could just tell Seth the truth this once . . .

"Put it this way," she said at last. "I'm not quite ready to stop pretending."

When she left the bus station, Diana drove straight to Adam's. He was waiting for her on the front porch when she pulled up.

"How about a walk?" he said as she got out of the car.

"Where's Summer?"

"After you called, I told her she could have the day off. I think she went over to town."

Diana took the handles of his wheelchair. "How do you push this thing?"

"It's motorized," Adam said, zipping past her down the ramp and into the driveway. He stopped and turned to face her, his smile almost hidden in the layers of bandages. "I know how you love to control things, Diana. Sorry."

Diana fell into step beside him. The day was crystalline, almost too bright.

"So," Adam said softly, "what gave it away?"

"The ring. I was there at Ross's birthday party when your dad gave it to him. Remember?"

Adam groaned. "*Now* I do. Damn, I should have known. I figured Summer wouldn't recognize it, since she barely knew Ross and he hardly ever wore the ring." He held out his hand. "It *is* kind of ostentatious. But I've worn it ever since Ross died, and I didn't feel right about taking it off. Don't ask me why."

"How long did you think you could keep up this charade, Adam? Summer was bound to find out eventually."

"I know, I know. It just . . . it just happened. I was already using a fake name, and then when she walked through the door that day to apply for the job, it was too good to be true. I had a little part of my old life back, you know?"

They turned toward the beach, going as far as Adam dared with the wheelchair. Diana sat beside him in the hot, sugar-fine sand.

"I knew your dad pretty well," she said. "And I hated him for the way he treated me after the stuff with Ross. But I have a hard time believing even the almighty Senator Merrick could dump you here under an assumed name when you were in this"—she gestured toward him with her hand—"this condition. I mean, sure, he didn't mind trying to destroy *me* if it meant saving his rear. But you're his son, Adam. I thought loyalty was everything to the Merrick clan." She couldn't leave a trace of bitterness out of her voice. "After all, when I needed you, Adam, you chose Ross over me."

Awkwardly Adam twisted his body toward

her. The bandages forced her to look directly into his eyes—it was as if there were nowhere else to look. And his eyes were so sad, it was almost more than Diana could stand.

"Yes, we've always been big on loyalty," Adam said. "But I guess even the almighty Senator Merrick couldn't put a good press spin on Ross and me. One son drunk and drowned. The other one nearly dead and also, for the record, quite drunk most of the time. Talk about your family values." Adam made a soft sound, like a laugh dissolving into a sob. "I guess you think I got what I deserved, huh, Diana? Poetic justice to the max."

"No. I don't hate you anymore, Adam. The truth is, what your family did to me made me stronger. I wouldn't wish it on anyone, but I'm still here. I survived, and I'm tougher for it."

She hesitated, watching the waves come and go. Gently, slowly, she reached for his left hand and held it, covering Ross's ring. "You'll be stronger too, when this is over."

"Maybe."

"You have to tell Summer, you know."

"I know. I've known all along. I just hate to see her quit, it was so nice having her around. Like going back in time." He paused. "She will leave, won't she?"

"It's hard to say. Summer's okay. She might just stick around."

Adam closed his fingers around hers. "How about you? You think you might, you know . . . stop back and say hi now and then?"

"I don't know, Adam," Diana said honestly. "I'm strong, but I'm not sure I'm strong enough to forget everything that happened."

"That's okay. I don't blame you."

"Maybe, though," Diana added softly.

They started back toward the house. When she reached her car, Diana paused. "So you'll tell her soon?"

"Soon, I promise. I just want to hang on to the illusion a little longer, okay?"

Diana nodded. "I understand. As it happens, I'm pretty good at make-believe myself."

24

You Can Go Home Again

After Jared gave her the day off, Summer spent a couple of hours just walking the beach, trying her best not to think too much. There was only one place she wanted to go, but it wasn't really home, not anymore.

After a while she headed for town. When she peeked through the window of Jitters, the café was nearly empty. Austin was wiping down a table.

She pushed open the door. "Table for one," she said, "if you can squeeze me in. I don't have a reservation."

"Right this way, mademoiselle."

He seated Summer by the window, then straddled a chair across from her. "You're looking radiant," he said.

"I'm feeling pretty radiant, actually."

"Marquez told me how things went down with Diver. I'm glad."

"I couldn't have done it without your apartment."

"Hey, I got my laundry folded. Too bad it was dirty."

"Eww."

"Just kidding. I think."

She reached into her pocket. "Before I forget. Your key."

"Maybe you should keep it. Just in case we decide to cohabit."

"Maybe I shouldn't."

"Hey, it was worth a shot." Austin lowered his voice. "By the way, Blythe told me Caroline's developed this sudden, inexplicable desire to head back to college early."

"Good. She'll be close by in case the cops need to question her. Diver's flying up to Virginia at the end of the week to work things out. My dad's paying for the ticket and meeting him there." She smiled. "Strange. It may do more to help cement their relationship than all those awkward father-son football tosses in our backyard."

"So." Austin crossed his arms. "Any other reason for the radiance?"

Summer reached into her purse and passed Austin her acceptance letter. He smiled broadly as he read it.

"Congratulations. I'm not surprised, of course. This is the right thing for you, Summer."

"I hope so." She put the letter away. "I'm scared to death. I'm going solo. No spotters. No net."

"You'll have friends nearby." Austin gazed at her, suddenly serious. "You'll have me."

"I've been thinking a lot about that, Austin," Summer said. "I—I told Seth good-bye. I told him I loved you."

"A wise choice indeed. I knew you'd come to your—"

"I also told him," Summer pressed on, "that I need to be by myself for a while. I need to figure out who I am and know I can get by on my own. To not be part of a couple. Not Summer and Austin. Just Summer."

Austin gazed at her, his face solemn, slowly, almost imperceptibly nodding.

"It's funny," Summer said, trying to fill the quiet with words, "when I first came here to the Keys, all I wanted in the world was to be part of a couple. I thought that was the only thing that mattered in the whole world. I still think it matters. Being in love is the most wonderful"—she smiled—"and the most wonderfully frustrating thing in the world. But I think it only works if you know what you want out of life. So you don't get lost in the other person."

She paused. Austin was still staring at her. "Well?" she said.

"Well, I want to tell you that you've just made a really lousy decision," Austin replied. "But I'm not going to. Because although it really hurts to admit this, Summer, I think you're probably right." He smiled, a slow smile that started at the corners of his mouth. "I think it's cool that you're brave enough to go solo for a while. And to do it at a place like Carlson, a place that scares you. It's the kind of thing that just makes me love you that much more." He laced his fingers behind his head, surveying her with affectionate annoyance. "Which is a drag, you see. I love you because you're stubborn and willful and independent, but of course it's exactly those qualities that are getting in the way of me sweeping you off your feet with my incredible charm."

"Oh, you swept me pretty good, Austin."

"This is just for a while, right? This isn't like some freaky hermit thing where you've sworn off human companionship till the end of time?"

"I'm sure we'll still run into each other. Even freaky hermits go to the movies now and then."

Austin sighed. "I told myself I would leave this in the hands of fate. And it appears fate has spoken. That bastard really gets on my nerves sometimes." He leaned across the table and kissed her sweetly. "But I can wait. I have a whole lot of *Baywatch*es on tape. And I figure you'll come to your senses eventually."

"It could happen." She stood. "Hey, before I go, could you load me up with three sticky buns and three orange juices to go?"

"Sure. Where are you off to?"

Summer smiled. "In search of some human companionship."

The apartment was quiet. Diana's door was closed, and so was Marquez's. Summer put the food from Jitters on the kitchen counter. She made as much noise as possible, searching for plates and forks.

Both doors opened at the same time.

"Summer?" Marquez cried.

"Summer?" Diana said. "What are you doing here?"

Summer placed the plates on the coffee table. "Hey, I paid a third of the rent—I have rights."

"Are you moving back in?" Marquez asked hopefully.

Summer shrugged. "I just wanted a little company, is all. Girl talk." She smiled. "Human companionship."

"And *Diana* came to mind?" Marquez sneered.

Summer sat cross-legged on the floor and grabbed a fork. She patted the couch. "Come on, you guys. They're still warm. Sit."

Diana and Marquez looked at each other warily.

"I promise to intervene if there's a significant loss of blood," Summer said. "Come on. Let's just hang out and talk. Like the old days."

"I don't know," Diana said, leaning against the counter. "It's been a long, hard summer. What can we all possibly agree on to talk about that won't lead to armed combat?"

"Guys?" Marquez suggested.

"No way," Diana and Summer said at the same moment.

"Food?" Summer suggested, holding up her plate.

"Pass," Marquez said.

"I have an idea," Diana said. "Let's talk about this fall. I caught another roach this morning the size of Nevada. I love this apartment, but if Summer's going to be at Carlson, and Marquez and I are going to be right down the road at FCU, I was thinking maybe we could look for something a little less roach infested when our lease is up. . . ." Her voice trailed off. "Sorry. We're not exactly ready for that, are we?"

Summer looked at Marquez. She looked at Diana. She smiled.

"Go get the want ads," she said.

About the Author

After Katherine Applegate graduated from college, she spent time waiting tables, typing (badly), watering plants, wandering randomly from one place to the next with her boyfriend, and just generally wasting her time. When she grew sufficiently tired of performing brain-dead minimum-wage work, she decided it was time to become a famous writer. Anyway, a writer. Writing proved to be an ideal career choice, as it involved neither physical exertion nor uncomfortable clothing, and required no social skills.

Ms. Applegate has written over sixty books under her own name and a variety of pseudonyms. She has no children, is active in no organizations, and has never been invited to address a joint session of Congress. She does, however, have an evil, foot-biting cat named Dick, and she still enjoys wandering randomly from one place to the next with her boyfriend.